This book belongs to:
Janie Clinton

1.00

D0873984

DOUBLE FEATURE

Double Feature

by

ROSAMOND DU JARDIN

J. B. LIPPINCOTT COMPANY

PHILADELPHIA AND NEW YORK

Contents

DOUBLE FEATURE

1 *A Very Small Wedding*

GRAN said, laughter deepening the web of fine lines at the corners of her bright blue eyes, "In view of the fact that it's going to be such a small wedding, I can't see why you're all running around in circles, getting into such a dither over it."

"Dither, she says!" Pam Howard regarded her grandmother with a fine imitation of severity, then swung back to the mirror to adjust the little lacy half-moon of hat on her dark head.

"It's all very well for her to talk." Pam's twin sister, Penny, craned her neck to see into the mirror over Pam's shoulder. "She's just the bride."

Gran chuckled, standing there in the doorway of the girls' pleasant maple-and-checked-gingham bedroom. Gran was a symphony in soft gray-blue, from the smart hat that topped her white head to the matching high-heeled pumps on her trim small feet. Gran's figure was frankly plump, but her sheer dress fitted well and brought

3

out the color of her eyes and accented her fresh clear complexion.

"Look at her," Pam said to Penny in a whisper meant for Gran's ears as well. "She looks perfectly gorgeous and in less than an hour she'll be Mrs. Lucius Hancock. But does that give her any right to stand there gloating over us poor spinsters?"

"My heart bleeds for you." Gran shook her head in mock sympathy. "Eighteen and not married yet." She turned away from the door, announcing as she left, "I'd better go see how your mother's getting along. As my Pennsylvania Dutch ancestors used to say, she's as much up in a heavel as you two are. You'd think no one ever got married before."

Pam's laughing gray glance met Penny's in the dresser mirror. "It isn't every day your grandmother does, though," she confided.

Penny laughed, too. But then she said, sobering, "Do you realize how dreadfully we're going to miss her? Even if she does live right here in Glenhurst, it won't be like having her in the same house with us."

"I know," Pam nodded. "If it were anyone but Lucius, I'd hate him for taking her away. But he's such an old dear."

"Like one of the family," Penny agreed.

They left it at that. Penny stooped to adjust a stocking seam, then moved away from the dresser in a swirl of sheer yellow skirts that crackled beguilingly with the taffeta petticoat beneath. She caught up the tiny white lace hat, a duplicate of Pam's, from the bed. The twins were dressed just alike for their grandmother's wedding, although they didn't go in for identical clothes nearly so much as they had when they were younger. It had been Penny's idea to stop the practice, since it so often led to their being mistaken for each other. Penny hadn't liked that, although Pam used to think it was sort of fun.

A faint reminiscent smile curved Pam's lips as her glance followed her sister in the mirror. Penny moved away with a kind of inverted Alice-through-the-looking-glass effect. Her dark hair was so much like Pam's own, their features, the slender roundness of their young figures were so similar, it was almost like seeing oneself in duplicate. Yet there were subtle differences of expression, even of bone structure in the shape of brow and chin, that made each girl easily identifiable to those who knew them well.

No one's got us mixed up in quite awhile, Pam thought a shade wistfully. It sort of spoils the fun of being twins.

It had been so different when they first moved to Glenhurst. Then they were forever being taken for each other. People weren't used to them, they hadn't had time to note the small details that set each girl apart. Soon their new acquaintances had realized that Pam was the one who talked a lot, who laughed and was at ease with everyone. Penny was more quiet and serious, not so sure of herself. Pam had led and Penny had followed, stumbling a little sometimes, not too happy or at home in the midst of the gay, smooth crowd of which Pam immediately became a part.

But the year just past had brought about a distinct change in Penny. No one was more aware of that than Pam. Penny had gradually loosed the bonds of Pam's loving and unintentional domination. She had learned to stand on her own feet and make her own friends, people who shared her likes and interests, which were quite different than her sister's. The climax of her new independence had come on the night of the senior prom, when Penny had been elected Prom Queen by the vote of the entire student body, while Pam had been merely one of her court of attendants.

But Pam hadn't minded, after the first shock of surprise. She had been glad for Penny, sincerely proud of her triumph. Knowing that she was well liked had been so good for her, had done wonders for her still not too strong self-confidence. Moreover, Penny's emergence as a person in her own right had brought the twins closer, somehow, than before. And all during the remainder of their last year at high school, through the fun and festivities attendant upon graduation, a warmth of mutual respect had augmented the natural affection they had always felt for each other.

It was only in fleeting, infrequent moments such as this that Pam found herself looking backward with a faint and wholly unreasonable nostalgia toward the old days when Penny had clung to and depended upon her, asking her advice, following it without question.

A year ago, Pam realized, Penny wouldn't have had an idea as to how to go about getting a boy really interested in her. Now Penny had Mike. A kind of tightness came up in Pam's throat as the picture of Mike Bradley moved across the screen of her mind. Mike was tall and Viking-blond, with blue eyes equally adapted to narrow with laughter or penetrate almost too deeply. Mike had been editor of the *Glen Crier*, a big wheel in half a dozen student activities. He could have had any girl to whom he

crooked an encouraging finger. And there had been a
time when Pam had wanted him badly, but Mike had
chosen Penny.

Pam felt a warmth of inner humiliation creep across
her face at the memories crowding in upon her. Once
Mike's attentions had been hers for the taking and Penny
had only hovered like a vague wistful shadow on the edge
of their association. But Mike had been just one of a
crowd of boys then, so far as Pam was concerned, along
with Randy Kirkpatrick, Spark Matthews, Joe Henderson.
Pam couldn't remember a time when she hadn't had
several boys sharing her time and attention. She felt no
undue pride in the thought, it was just the way things
were. There had never been a dance at school when she
didn't have her choice of dates for it. Boys liked Pam and
she liked them. She could twist them around her fingers,
make them do as she wanted. Penny had never been able
to understand how she did it. Still, by the time Pam had
realized that Mike was rather more important to her than
the others, she had lost her chance with him. He had
turned to Penny and they had become deeply interested
in each other. The feeling between them ran strong and
sure and Pam was the one left out, hovering on the
sidelines.

Not that she hovered noticeably. She still had more
dates than she could well handle. Randy Kirkpatrick,
dark and rather quiet, but attractive and wealthy, was
always taking her places, dropping in to see her, seeking
her company at every opportunity. Pam was fond of
Randy, they had lots of fun. But sometimes, seeing Penny
and Mike together, a queer lost feeling of emptiness

caught at Pam. As though she had missed something warm and sweet and vital that had once been almost within her grasp.

Her sister's voice broke into her thoughts, asking, "If we're both all ready, why don't we go help Mother?"

But Celia Howard's quiet laugh sounded from the doorway before Pam could answer. "Never mind. I'm just as ready as you are."

The twins turned to look at her and admiring smiles curved their mouths. Mother wore a dusty rose shantung suit in a soft feminine style that did flattering things for her still slim figure and pretty face. The gray in her crisply curly hair only made it seem more blond under her rose-colored hat with its little puff of veil.

Penny exclaimed, "How nice you look!"

And Pam nodded agreement. "Perfectly scrumptious!"

The sudden realization struck her of how very much Mother would miss Gran. They'd all miss her, of course, but Mother most of all. Gran had willingly taken over the details of cooking and housekeeping, so that Celia could devote her full attention to managing Howard House, the interior decorating shop that supported them all. Mother had bought the big old house and remodeled it into the shop, with living quarters above, secure in the expectation that Gran would stay on with them, just as she had for so many years. Yet it was obvious that Mother was wholeheartedly delighted over Gran's imminent marriage. She was putting Gran's happiness ahead of her own convenience, just as she always put the twins' needs and desires before her own.

Maybe, Pam thought in a moment of rare insight, it's because she knows how lonely it is to be a widow.

Her glance lingered thoughtfully on her mother's face.

Then Gran spoke, in her brisk, dry way, from the hallway behind Celia. "Well, don't just stand there, all of you. We haven't got all day, you know."

"Darling," Pam teased, "brides aren't supposed to sound so anxious."

"I'm not going to keep Lucius waiting," Gran said firmly. "This sort of thing is hard enough on a man his age without making him all nervous and upset because I'm late."

"You're cute," Pam said, flying to give Gran a hug.

And Penny, too, came to press her cheek briefly against Gran's and assure her, "Of course, you mustn't keep him waiting."

Gran put an arm around each of them, her blue eyes suspiciously bright. "I'm going to miss you two, pesky as you are," she said. "Just goes to show a person can get used to anything."

Mother said, "It won't seem natural around here without you."

"I'll only be a few blocks away." Gran's tone was calm, but feeling quivered underneath. "As soon as we get back from the Ozarks, we'll be seeing almost as much of you as ever."

Mother nodded, as though she didn't quite trust herself to speak. Pam felt a curious thickness in her own throat and, glancing at Penny, she sensed that her sister, too, was struggling to keep her innermost emotions from showing too plainly.

"Why don't we all break down and have a good cry?" Pam suggested drily.

The absurd remark cleared the air just as she had hoped

it would. A burst of laughter relieved the tension that had threatened to build up too disturbingly. Penny squeezed her arm gratefully and Mother's brief look was warm with appreciation.

And Gran said, still chuckling, "Trust Pam to keep things from getting too sticky."

Just then they heard the downstairs door open and the voice of Dorothea Crane, Mother's good friend and assistant in the shop, call out, "Hello, up there. Anybody ready?"

That meant that Dorothea had the Howard House station wagon parked out in front. She had promised to come and get them in plenty of time.

"We're coming," Mother said, her voice almost as natural as though they had a wedding in the family every day.

Afterward, Pam couldn't remember too much about the brief, moving ceremony in the small chapel of their church. There were tall white flowers at the altar. The dozen or so guests filled only a few front pews. Mike Bradley and Randy Kirkpatrick were there, along with Randy's parents and a few other couples, friends of Gran's and Lucius' from Glenhurst and Chicago.

Light fell softly through the stained glass windows as the minister's deep voice began, "Dearly beloved, we are gathered here . . ."

Was Gran remembering, Pam wondered, those same words falling on her ears so many, many years ago, when she had married the twins' grandfather? He had been dead so long now and Gran was no longer young. But the words must be the same, the measured enduring words of the marriage ceremony. Pam tried to concentrate on the service, but her thoughts kept skipping off on the oddest tangents. Lucius was such a dear, but it would be quite strange to have to call him Grandfather. Or would he expect that, she wondered. He looked almost unfamiliar, standing there so erect and solemn in his welltailored dark suit. Usually Lucius' taste ran more to colorful sport shirts and baggy slacks. Pam felt a bubble of laughter burst within her, speculating whether Lucius had his smelly old pipe tucked away in a pocket of his proper suit.

She sobered abruptly then, watching him slip the ring on Gran's finger. What would it be like, Pam wondered, to be a bride, to be getting married, not when you were old like Gran, but when you were young and filled with crowding, turbulent feelings?

Her glance slipped sideways to Penny's face, but Penny was so intent on the proceedings, she didn't notice. Was Penny, too, thinking about being a bride? Was she dreaming of marrying Mike, of repeating the slow, sweet words, "I, Penny, take thee, Michael . . ." and feeling Mike's hand shake a little as he put the ring on her finger?

Pam's throat felt chokey and her eyelids stung. But it was so corny to cry at weddings. She wouldn't do it. She wouldn't!

And then the organ music came up in a great swell and the wedding was over. And she hadn't cried—quite. The minister shook hands with Gran and Lucius and they came briskly back down the aisle, beaming and happy. Everyone crowded around them at the back of the chapel and there was laughter and kissing and congratulations.

Pam and Penny started whispering to each other just before Mike and Randy came up to them, confessing in practically the same words, "I almost cried—" They broke off, their glances locking, laughter easing the thickness in both their throats.

And Mike Bradley said, approaching, "Look at them, giggling their heads off. Don't you two know that weddings are very serious occasions?"

"Why, no," Pam said, pulling her gaze from Mike's face to flash Randy a welcoming smile, "nobody told us."

2   *Afterthoughts*

THE wedding reception was held at home in the comfortable second floor apartment above Howard House. Both Gran and Lucius had preferred it so, liking informality and the easy privacy of familiar surroundings. A local caterer took charge of the details, so that Mother didn't have to do a thing, except to be the gracious hostess, which came quite naturally to her.

Everything tasted delicious. Chicken salad and crisp buttery little rolls, ice cream and the wedding cake, decorated with lovely white sugar roses. There was much laughter and advice to Gran and Lucius as to just how to cut the cake. There were toasts drunk in the clear, bubbly champagne which the Kirkpatricks had brought.

Pam didn't like the taste of the champagne very much. It made her nose tickle and felt almost sour going down her throat. But it engendered a pleasant after-warmth, a feeling of airy happiness. And she liked seeing the bubbles rise like a miniature fountain through the hollow stems of Mother's fragile glasses.

Randy murmured into her ear, standing close beside

13

her and lifting his glass toward her before drinking, "Here's to us."

"To us," Pam smiled and took a small sip.

But Randy didn't smile. His glance remained grave, almost brooding, on her face. Pam felt a little uncomfortable under his look. More and more often lately Randy's attitude toward her made her feel uncomfortable. Sometimes he looked at her so seriously, sometimes he said such solemn things, it was disturbing. She liked Randy well enough, she had always enjoyed being with him, but she wasn't, by any stretch of the imagination, in love with him. And she had been troubled by the recurrent suspicion in recent weeks that he might be falling a little in love with her.

Oh, dear, Pam thought, that would complicate things!

She laughed up at Randy, demanding, "Why are we drinking to us? Gran's the bride and Lucius is the bridegroom. They're the ones to drink to."

"I already did," Randy said. And Pam was relieved when his slow, rather wry grin lighted his face. "So now I'm drinking to the bride's granddaughter and me. Anything wrong with that?"

Pam shook her head. With this Randy she felt quite at ease. It was only with the brooding dark stranger who sometimes seemed to stare out of his eyes that she wasn't sure of her ground.

Penny and Mike came up to them then and the conversation became four-cornered and trivial. Pam found herself hoping that they wouldn't drift off in the crowd again, leaving her alone with Randy. But that was absurd, Pam told herself. How could you be alone with anyone in the midst of a milling crowd of people at a gay wedding reception?

The big high-ceilinged rooms echoed with talk and laughter until Gran and Lucius left. Everyone hurried down the stairs before the departing couple, to throw rice and call out farewells and best wishes and then, as the red tail-light of Lucius' sleek new car grew smaller and disappeared into the night, to troop back upstairs, or homeward through the fragrant June darkness. None of the guests lingered much longer. There were faint bluish shadows under Mother's eyes, with the strain and excitement of it all. The Kirkpatricks and Randy and Mike were the last to go and then, with the door shut, there were only the twins and Celia left and the apartment was suddenly too quiet.

"Well," Mother said, sitting down on the couch and kicking off her high-heeled slippers, "that's that." The smile she gave her daughters was just a little tremulous.

Penny collapsed beside her, enjoying a luxurious stretch. "Everything went off perfectly," she said. "It was a lovely wedding."

Pam perched on the arm of a chair, dangling one stockinged foot and yawning. "It certainly was," she agreed. "Everyone said so. You know," she admitted with the complete frankness that was a part of her charm, "I was afraid it would seem—well, sort of queer. I mean a wedding where the bride and groom were so old. But it didn't. They were sweet, both of them."

Mother nodded. "I thought so, too. And they're so right for each other. I know they'll be happy. Old age must be very lonely, all alone as Lucius was."

Penny put in, "He doesn't expect us to call him Grandfather. He told me so. He said Lucius is perfectly all right."

"Were you worried about that, too?" Pam asked with a little laugh. "I got to thinking about it during the ceremony."

"I got to worrying about whether Gran had remembered to change her old wide wedding ring to her right hand," Penny admitted. "But she had. And isn't her new ring gorgeous?"

"All those diamonds," Pam agreed. "Lucius must have more money than we realized, getting a new car and all, too."

Mother laughed. "Is that a nice way to speculate about your new grandfather's financial standing?"

"We just want to be sure he's got enough to support Gran in the manner to which she's accustomed," Pam said, laughing, too. "It's not that we're mercenary."

"I don't think you have to worry about it," Mother said. "In fact, right now I'm too tired to worry about anything. I'm going to bed."

"Me, too," Penny agreed, yawning.

Mother asked casually as she got up and began turning off lamps, "Didn't I hear Mike and Randy suggesting that you go for a little ride?"

Pam nodded. "We were too tired, though."

Mother stopped and stood there, one hand resting on a light switch, her blue glance penetrating on her daughter's face. "You're sure?"

"Sure of what?" Pam asked innocently.

"That you were too tired to go," Mother said. "That it wasn't just that you didn't want to leave me alone, for fear I'd get all morbid and weepy over Gran's leaving?"

"Why, of course not," Penny said.

And Pam echoed, "What a weird idea!"

Mother stood there, a slow smile spreading gradually across her face. "Fakers!" she said fondly.

"Who, us?" Pam gulped.

"Never mind the act," Mother said. "It was very sweet of you both. And you know what? I'm glad you stayed home with me. There'll be plenty of other nights for going riding. And happy as I honestly am over Gran's marriage—well, I might have felt just a bit martyred if you and all the wedding guests had gone off and left me here alone. Because I am going to miss her very much. I can't truthfully deny that."

"We all will," Penny said. "Why, Gran's been with us since Pam and I were ten years old, since—" her voice trailed off and she went over and put her arm around Mother.

"Since Rick was killed," Celia Howard said simply, her voice low. And then she said, her eyes gentle on Penny's face, "Don't ever hesitate to speak of your father, dear. When someone is gone from your life, it helps to keep him near if you talk of him sometimes."

And so they lingered for a moment, discussing Richard Howard, who had died eight years before in a skidding car. Memories came crowding all about them, but Mother's memories must have been richer, fuller-bodied than those of the twins, because Rick had been her husband. Pam's and Penny's memories of their father were misty, vague. A half-recalled look or gesture. The way a tall thin man had stooped so readily to play with them, his habit of lighting a match for his cigarette with a flick of a fingernail, the droll, fantastic stories he had told them as he tucked them into bed.

"Always remember," Mother said, "that he was the kindest man in the world and that he loved us all dearly. He would have liked to see you two grow up; he'd have been proud of you, just as I am. Sometimes," she added, her tone rueful, "I've felt it isn't quite fair to you, living in such a female sort of household. You miss a lot."

"We're one female less now," Pam reminded. "And at least there's a grandfather in the family."

"So there is," Mother said, with a little smile.

They turned off the rest of the lights and headed for bed. But after the twins had kissed Mother good-night and had gone into their own room, Pam still felt too keyed up and excited to settle down and sleep. Penny put on her pajamas and creamed her face and got into bed, while Pam still sat on the little slip-covered stool before the dressing table, fiddling with her nail polish, brushing her hair, re-arranging the perfume bottles.

"For creep's sake," Penny said finally, "are you going to stay up all night?"

"I might," Pam said. "I'm just in the mood for it."

"Come to bed," Penny coaxed. "Aren't you tired? I am."

"Yes and no," Pam said maddeningly. "My feet are tired but inside I feel just like that champagne looked in the glasses, full of little rising bubbles. Penny, don't you ever feel—oh, full of questions that you don't know the answers to, and sort of impatient to be all grown-up and mature and at the same time just a little scared at the idea?"

"Sure, I do," Penny said, raising herself on one elbow to stare at Pam. "That is, I don't know the answers to all my questions and I'm anxious to be grown-up, but I can't say I'm exactly scared."

"Sometimes I am," Pam admitted.

"Why?" Penny asked. "What are you afraid of?"

"That's one of the questions I don't know the answer to," Pam said.

"Go to sleep," Penny murmured drowsily.

But Pam still sat at the dressing table, thinking. She wondered if the reason the future didn't frighten Penny was because she had Mike. Maybe, if you were really crazy about each other, as Penny and Mike were, it made things more sure and solid than when you hadn't made up your mind about a boy yet. There were several Pam liked and who seemed to like her. At least, they called up often and took her places. Pam had to confess, when she thought about it, that she liked different boys for different reasons. Randy because he was attractive and had plenty of money to spend. Spark Matthews because he was, or had been, captain of the football team and a big man around high school. Joe Henderson because he was so funny and full of pep that ever so many girls had a yen for him. And there were others and would be more, Pam thought with the easy confidence of a girl who had always had more boys hovering around her than she had time for. After this summer there'd be college, if Mother could swing it financially. Pam crossed her fingers automatically and hoped that business continued good at Howard House. She and Penny hadn't yet decided where they were going. But whichever college they chose, there'd be boys there. A whole new crop of boys, Pam reflected, deriving some satisfaction from the thought. And surely, among so many, she'd find a special one.

In the meantime, there was this summer stretching ahead. And there were Randy and Spark and Joe and the others. If she could just keep Randy from getting too serious, from deciding he wanted to monopolize her time, as Mike monopolized Penny's—Pam's thought broke and splintered into the realization that it would be an altogether different thing to be monopolized by Mike. She glanced across the room at her sister. Penny had already fallen asleep. Her face looked young and serene against the plump whiteness of the pillow. One hand was curled under her cheek.

Penny had known from the very beginning that Mike was the one she wanted. And she had won his interest and affection by being herself, by breaking free of her dependence on Pam.

But Pam remembered, I could have had him once.

And the feeling of emptiness and loss, of unfulfillment, grew into an actual pain within her . . .

3
The
Splash Party

"HONESTLY," Pam moaned, swishing the dish cloth distastefully over the scouring powder she had just sprinkled on the sink, "I had no idea how much work Gran must have done."

"Didn't you?" A faint grin lifted the corners of Penny's mouth as she dried a saucer. "I knew it was plenty. Only Gran never seemed to mind. I think she enjoys housework."

"Well, I don't," Pam said flatly.

"Some I don't mind," Penny admitted. "Dishwashing I could live without. But the rest of it isn't too bad."

"You can have it," Pam said. "All of it."

The warm mid-day sunshine falling through the window above the sink reminded her abruptly that she didn't have too much time. Laurie McGregor's splash party at the country club pool was scheduled for two o'clock and it must be after one right this minute.

Pam tossed the dish cloth crookedly on the towel rack

and told her twin, "I've got to rush. Randy's picking me up at a quarter to. And I haven't had my shower yet and my nails are a mess. Look," she held up her slightly pinkened fingers for Penny's inspection. "Dishpan hands."

"It's just from the hot water," Penny pointed out. "A little lotion will fix it up. Anyway, everybody has to do dishes sometimes. That's life."

But Pam shook her head positively. "Laurie doesn't."

The McGregors were as rich, maybe even richer, than the Kirkpatricks, Pam thought, as she hurried into the bathroom and began stripping for her shower. Randy and his parents lived in a great English-style house on Park Lane, one of Glenhurst's nicest residential streets. And Randy had an old convertible, which he always referred to drily as his "heap." But the McGregors had recently built a dreamy sprawling brick ranch house not far from the country club, with acres of beautifully tended grounds, complete with stone terraces, a three-car attached garage and a stable in back for a couple of blooded saddle horses.

Pam sighed a small heartfelt sigh, just thinking of all the wonderful things Laurie McGregor had and took entirely for granted. The little English roadster that had been her graduation gift, the beautiful, unostentatiously expensive clothes, the generous amount of spending money. Pam's thoughts centered wistfully on Laurie's possessions as the warm needles of water splashed down around her shoulders.

She made an effort to shut off her thoughts, as she reached out to twist the shower dial. But the water slowed and stopped in obedience to her wishes, while her musings ran on rebelliously. Oh, well, might as well be philosophical about it, Pam admonished herself. It was only money, as the saying went. And even though Laurie had so much and was a very attractive girl besides, she hadn't been able to hang onto Randy Kirkpatrick. He used to be her steady date before the Howards moved to Glenhurst.

"But now he's mine," Pam murmured aloud, and felt a very human sense of satisfaction.

Why shouldn't Laurie, who had practically everything, lose Randy to someone else? Pam strongly suspected that Laurie was only friendly with her because she was too proud to want people to think she was jealous.

A little smile curled Pam's mouth as she toweled herself briskly dry. She didn't care, actually, why Laurie was friendly toward her, why she invited her to her parties. "So long as she does," Pam told her reflection in the medicine cabinet mirror with a little chuckle . . .

Later, lying beside Randy on cushioned pads at the edge of the club pool, Pam felt lazy and luxurious. She loved the country club and all it stood for. The white-painted brick clubhouse with its shaded terrace and thick-carpeted lounge, the flower-bordered paths and the azure-lined pool, the tennis courts and golf course—all of these things seemed in Pam's mind to be symbols of a way of life that approached perfection. Just being there gave her a sense of pleasure and importance. Maybe someday, if Howard House became a more and more successful enterprise, the Howards could afford to join the club. Pam had to smile a little at her own fantastic day-dreaming. Right now all Mother's efforts were bent on earning enough to let both twins start college in the fall. It would be a long time before they could afford any such grand gestures as joining the country club. And, in the mean-

time, since she got to come here often with Randy, or
Laurie, or some of the rest of the crowd, why should she
worry?

"A dime for your thoughts," Randy said, grinning at
her. "On account of inflation, you know?"

Pam grinned back. "Payment in advance," she said, "or
I won't tell you."

"You mean my credit's no good at a time like this?"
Randy demanded in mock indignation, slapping his wet
trunks.

"In that case," Pam smiled at him sweetly, "we'll make
an exception. I was just thinking how lucky I am to have
friends who invite me to elegant places like this."

"Oh," Randy said. "Was that all? I thought you might
have been thinking about something vital. Me, for
instance."

"You're one of my friends, aren't you?" Pam's tone
was teasing and there was a warmly personal note in it.

She wondered, Why do I automatically flirt with a boy,
even one I don't really want to encourage too much?

It was habit, actually, and Pam knew it. The right teasing easy words rose to her lips without her putting any
conscious thought on it. That was the way it was with
her. And the boys loved it, they flocked around to be
teased and flattered and flirted with, they ate it up and
begged for more—Pam's thought broke jerkily.

Not all boys, she reminded herself. Not Mike Bradley.

At first, though, Mike had been just like all the others.
Now he was Penny's and she was welcome to him, Pam
told herself. But the words carried no conviction, even in
her thoughts. She wished she could forget about Mike.
Maybe, if she concentrated very hard on Randy—

She proceeded to do just that all the rest of the golden afternoon. Laurie's party was lots of fun. They had delicious hamburgers at the pool's edge, served from a gleaming portable grill by a waiter. And there were tall tinkling glasses of limeade with sherbet and a variety of fancy cakes.

"We won't dare swim after this," Pam moaned.

And Randy chuckled, "We'd all sink for sure."

So they sat, lazy and surfeited, in the sunshine, talking and joking. The afternoon waned and the sun's rays slanted, lengthening the shadows about the pool. But no one felt like breaking up the party and going home. It was such fun to be young and gay and in congenial company.

Laurie McGregor asked, pushing her soft hair back from her eyes, "What's happened to Mike Bradley? I haven't seen him since school was out."

Pam said, "He's working. Didn't you know?"

"He's the workingest guy ever," Randy said with a grin. He and Mike were good friends, so he, too, knew what Mike was doing. "Days he drives Langan's delivery truck. And nights he works at the movie. I'm surprised you haven't seen him there."

"Who goes to the movies inside in the summer?" someone asked. "This is the drive-in season."

"It might be worth it to get to see Mike," Susan Farnsworth drawled, her dark eyes dancing impishly. "I miss him."

"You'd only be wasting your time," Laurie assured her. "Pam's twin has him all sewed up. Hasn't she?" Laurie asked then, her wide blue glance going from Susan to Pam.

"Oh, definitely," Pam nodded. "I can't even get him away from her myself."

There was laughter then, with Pam's laugh augmenting it. No one would have suspected she was half serious.

"Just don't let me catch you trying," Randy told her quizzically.

Susan Farnsworth inquired, "Was that why Penny didn't come today, because Mike couldn't be here?"

"She said she had to work," Laurie said.

Pam nodded. "We sort of take turns helping Mother in the shop. She has to be out a lot on jobs and Howard House has been so busy lately it's more than her assistant can handle."

She felt a faint warmth of color creep across her face. In her heart Pam knew that Penny worked in the shop a good deal more than she did. But Penny hadn't minded turning down Laurie's invitation, while to do so would have been a real sacrifice for Pam. Penny wasn't keen on going to the country club with Pam's crowd, especially when Mike couldn't be there. She had been quite willing for Pam to go, while she helped in the shop in Pam's place. Why, Penny might not have come to Laurie's party anyway, Pam thought defensively. And the feeling of shame, of having imposed on her twin, receded.

Someone noticed the time and a general exodus toward the locker-rooms and showers began. Afterward they all gathered on the clubhouse steps to tell each other "so long" and to thank Laurie. Randy and Pam gave Susan Farnsworth and Mitch Martin a lift home. It was Pam who offered to do so, but Randy didn't seem to mind.

Still, when they had dropped the others at their respective homes and were headed toward Howard House,

Randy told Pam, "Sometimes I get a queer hunch that you like me better in a crowd."

"Of all the crazy notions," Pam said lightly.

"Is it?" Randy's dark glance met hers briefly, probingly, then returned to the road ahead. "Then why do you always try to put off being alone with me as long as possible?"

"Because I offered Susan and Mitch a lift?" Pam demanded. "We couldn't just let them walk home, could we?"

"Someone else would have taken them if we hadn't," Randy said. "But it's not just Sue and Mitch I'm talking about. It's not just today. I've had this feeling for quite awhile, this idea that you're not too interested when there's just the two of us."

"Oh, Randy," Pam coaxed, "don't go being difficult and spoiling things when we've had such a grand afternoon. Didn't you enjoy it?"

"Sure," Randy said. "I had a swell time. You always treat me fine when we're with the crowd. It's different when we're alone, though."

"How different?"

"I don't know exactly," Randy admitted, frowning. "I get an idea you're kind of—putting me off someway, that you don't want to talk about anything important or serious."

"Randy," Pam said firmly, "you have too much imagination. That's your trouble." She went on in a gently patient, ingratiating tone, "I date you more than anyone else, don't I?"

"I guess so," Randy had to admit.

"And would I do that," Pam pressed, "if I didn't like

you? After all, you're not the only man in my life."

"You're telling me!" Randy's tone was wry. "Maybe that's why I worry."

"You needn't," Pam assured him. She leaned her head against his shoulder and the breeze blew her soft dark hair upward like a caress across his cheek. She could feel his shoulder relax a little, as though some tension, some pent-up resistance had gone out of him. Pam had never known a boy she couldn't get around if she just put her mind on it . . .

4 *College Is a Big Deal*

SUNDAY breakfast was a leisurely affair for the twins and their mother, to be eaten comfortably in robes and slippers before getting dressed for church. It was their best chance for talking over things that had happened, for discussing problems.

The food was always special, consisting of favorite dishes which hurried week-day mornings left no time for. This particular Sunday Celia, looking fresh and pretty in a pale blue housecoat, presided over the waffle iron. A spirited conversation was under way, touching on Penny's and Mike's plans for a trip into Chicago to the Field Museum that afternoon, Pam's enthusiastic description of the summer theater she had attended the previous night, and Celia's interested queries and comments on both subjects.

Penny said, helping herself to the maple syrup, "It's wonderful how many things you can do that are fun and interesting and still cost practically nothing."

"Museums," Pam's tone was lightly derisive. "Who wants to spend their time dragging around dumpy places like that?"

She wondered if Penny's professed enjoyment of such activities was real. Or did she simply have to pretend for Mike's sake? Mike was always so broke, his and Penny's dates had to cost very little. He was saving toward college, trying hard to get together enough before fall to pay his tuition and tide him over until he could line up a part-time job at school. Pam didn't know Mike's family very well, but she was aware, through Penny, that all the Bradleys' savings had been absorbed a few years before by medical expenses attendant upon the severe illness of one of Mike's two young sisters. Mike knew that any education beyond high school that he succeeded in getting would be squarely up to him. That was why he had taken on two jobs this summer.

Penny exclaimed, her tone sincere enough to convince anyone, "We love museums! There are so many different things so see, you never get bored. And afterwards we're going to eat at a little place on Rush Street, where they have absolutely fabulous spaghetti and then Mike has tickets for a radio broadcast."

Pam thought, And none of it will cost him a cent, except the train fare and the spaghetti. And Penny will be quite content and think she's had a marvelous time. How can she be like that?

The question hung unanswered in Pam's mind. In some ways she couldn't understand Penny at all. She knew well that she wouldn't be satisfied with dates spent in museums and taking in free radio broadcasts. Or with just movies or picnics or long walks or evenings at home listening to records. Those things were all right for an occasional date, but not very often. Things had to move at a faster, gayer tempo to keep Pam interested. With Randy there was always something new and different to do, some exciting and expensive place to go. He practically knocked himself out trying to please her.

Take last night for instance. Along with Sue Farnsworth and Mitch Martin, they had driven almost fifty miles to see a Hollywood star perform at a North Shore summer theater. And after the show they had eaten and danced at the Beach Walk and had driven home very late through the moonlit summer night.

Pam smiled a little, remembering what fun it had been. And yet, she realized honestly, it had been the things they did, the places they went, which had made the evening so exciting. With Mike beside her instead of Randy, it would all have been infinitely more enjoyable. But Mike couldn't afford to give her such an evening— and besides, Mike was Penny's . . .

Pam came back to the present at the sound of Mother's voice, saying warmly, "I've got some news for you two— good news."

Both girls looked at her inquiringly. Their mother's eyes moved from one young face to the other and there was a lilting note of pleasure in her voice as she told them, "I went over the Howard House books last night in detail. I've been afraid to promise you both that you could start college this fall, for fear I couldn't swing it. But now I'm sure I can."

"Oh, glory!" Pam exclaimed, feeling her heart lift.

And Penny said, her eyes lighting, "Oh, Mother, how wonderful! You're sure it won't be too hard for you?"

Celia Howard shook her head. "I know we can work it out," she said confidently. "Not one of the most expensive schools, but some smaller one, where the tuition and living costs won't be too steep."

"I like a small school better, anyway," Penny said.

And Pam agreed, "Lots of them sound wonderful in the catalogues. I've been afraid to even look at those too seriously, because then I'd get my hopes up and just die if we couldn't both go."

The pleasurable sense of relief within her swelled and bubbled. Penny was experiencing this same crazy intoxication of excitement and delight, Pam knew. Their glances flashed wordless messages back and forth to each other. Neither of them had talked much about it, but each had faced in her heart the possibility that only one of them might get to go to college this fall, while the other waited until next year, spending the intervening time helping Mother and Dorothea Crane with the work at Howard House. And Pam had realized that if a choice had to be made, Penny would be the logical one to go first. Penny was much the better student, she had got top grades in high school and had always applied herself to her studies much more conscientiously than Pam.

But, golly, Pam thought, college sounded like such fun! She wasn't sure she could have borne it to be the one left out. A whole new way of living, new friends, a different background. In her mind's eye, Pam saw a shining scene. Old stone walls with ivy clinging to them, broad paths bordering a velvet lawn. Couples in bright clothes, walking along arm in arm, the men all tall and handsome, the girls pretty and vivacious. Sorority and fraternity houses, bright-lit for parties in the gray dusk—

Pam's entranced thoughts broke of their own weight. "Gee," she exclaimed, laughing, "I guess I've been seeing too many college movies! I'm getting all starry-eyed and breathless."

"Me, too," Penny admitted, her grin a little wry. "And I'm so glad we can both go. I've known in the back of my mind all along that if we had to make a choice, Pam should get to go first."

Pam stared at her in astonishment. "I figured you should—and I wasn't sure I could take it."

"Oh, no," Penny shook her head. "You'd get so much more out of it—the social stuff and all. You'd make so many more friends."

"I'd have fun," Pam admitted frankly, "but I'm such a lousy student. Why, what would I do without you there to needle me into studying?"

Mother was smiling at them both, her blue glance pleased and proud. "I'm glad each of you figured the other would be the one. That makes it all the nicer for you to be able to go together. Unless—" a faint questioning note crept into her voice, "you'd prefer to go to different schools?"

"Oh, no!" the two short words exploded at her in two voices, equally appalled.

"We couldn't do that!" Pam added. "We've always been together."

And Penny said seriously, "If I still copied Pam the way I used to, it might be a good thing for us to separate. But it isn't necessary any longer."

"Of course it isn't," Mother agreed. "It's purely a

matter of choice for you both. Each of you can stand alone as an individual. And if you'll enjoy going to the same college—well, that's the thing to do."

Pam said, laughing, "Besides, think how many more clothes we'll have if we can pool our wardrobe!"

Penny nodded. "And it would be awful not to have Pam there to tell things to. We've confided in each other for years."

"We couldn't break the habit now," Pam said positively.

Mother admitted, smiling, "Somehow, I was pretty sure you'd feel like that. So now all you have to do is study those catalogues you've been collecting and find a school you can still get into that appeals to both of you—and that we can afford."

"Details," Pam said airily.

And Penny agreed confidently, "We'll find one."

But choosing a school proved to be far from a simple task, although the twins had narrowed the field down to three of four even before Mother gave them the go-ahead. Most of their friends were already enrolled at the schools of their choice. Only a few still remained undecided. College was the big deal that summer and talk of schools cropped up whenever any of the June graduates got together. They discussed heatedly and at length the respective merits of big universities and smaller schools, of co-ed institutions, of colleges that afforded the boys some sort of military service tie-in. Most of Pam's crowd would be attending well-known colleges in the East. Penny's cronies had picked smaller, Midwestern schools where expenses were somewhat lower.

Randy Kirkpatrick had little choice, actually. He had been slated for Cornell, his father's old school, for as long as he could remember. His grandfather had gone there, too.

"Just a victim of tradition," Mike Bradley cracked one day when Pam and Penny and Randy and he had got onto the fascinating subject of colleges for perhaps the hundredth time. "Doesn't it kind of take the fun out of it to have everything decided for you in advance?"

"Oh, I don't know," Randy argued. "It's certainly less bother and Cornell's a good school. And I didn't have to beat my brains trying to make up my mind like the rest of you."

The four of them had driven out to the woods for a Sunday afternoon picnic. Sunday and a couple of week-day evenings were the only time Mike had free. He sat now, his back braced comfortably against a slanting tree-trunk, his long legs thrust out. Penny sat beside him, her arms clasped around blue-jeaned knees, her glance warm on Mike's face.

Why must she look at him like that, Pam thought with a sharp thrust of impatience, as if he was so special?

She dropped her glance to the square of plaid table-cloth spread on the ground. Randy, sprawled on his elbows beside Pam, reached out to help himself to another olive. Only a few scattered remains of their lunch were still jumbled together on the cloth, some olives and potato chips and a couple of rejected sandwiches.

"That's half the fun," Mike told Randy, "making up your mind. Of course," he added with his swift grin that Pam looked up in time to see, "with me it isn't just a matter of which school 1 prefer. The question of where I'll have the best chance to earn some moola comes into it, too."

"You'll work it out," Randy said and there was a note of genuine admiration underneath his kidding banter. "I never knew such a guy for figuring the angles. Why, if you were set down on a campus where there wasn't a single job available, you'd have some kind of service dreamed up inside of twenty-four hours to sell the rest of the students at a profit."

"Thanks, pal," Mike chuckled. "I never knew you thought I was so smart."

"Not just smart," Randy corrected. "You're willing to work for your money. That makes you twice as sure to get by."

Pam said lazily, turning over on her back to lie staring up at the blue sky with its lacy pattern of leaves and branches, "Think of the fun he'll miss, though, having to grub along at a job in his spare time."

"Okay, lily of the field," Randy said, reaching out to tousle her hair affectionately, "that's about enough out of you."

"I mean it," Pam said. "It's the extracurricular side of college I'm looking forward to."

"You would," Mike told her. "You'll probably go in so heavily on the social stuff you'll get flunked out."

"Oh, Penny wouldn't let that happen to me." Pam rolled back onto her tummy to smile at her twin. "I can count on her."

"You're telling us?" Mike cracked. "Personally, I couldn't see why they didn't just give Penny two high school diplomas and be done with it."

Pam threw a sandwich crust at him and Mike caught it and tossed it to some patiently waiting sparrows nearby.

"All the time insults!" Pam exclaimed, laughing. "Can I help it if I'm not a brain like Penny?"

"I'm not a brain, either," Penny denied. "I'm just not allergic to studying. But we'll both have to buckle down in college. It's lots harder than high school."

Pam said lightly, "Oh, I'll get by. I guess you have to keep your grades up to a certain level to be pledged by a sorority."

"You see how her mind runs?" Randy said fondly. "Baby, let me clue you. The main object of college is to impart knowledge and develop your thinking power, not just offer you a four-year binge of fun and gayety and l'amour."

The good-natured raillery went on. Mike helped himself to a generous handful of potato chips. He fed a couple to Penny, then pulled her close against him, so that she lay in the easy circle of his arm, her head on his shoulder. Pam's expression didn't alter, seeing them so, but something dark and ugly twisted within her. And she pulled away impatiently from Randy's caressing hand and made little stabbing motions with a twig at the grass in front of her.

Mike said thoughtfully after a time, "I've just about made up my mind to go to Harwood. It's in my price range and the job opportunities are tops. And there are a couple of English professors there it would be a privilege to work with."

Mike wanted to write, or to teach English, Pam knew. And Penny, too, was interested in writing.

Now she said, immediately enthusiastic, "I think I

like Harwood best, too."

Pam glanced at her in surprise. It was the first time she had heard Penny express such a positive preference. Harwood was one of the schools they were still considering, but Pam was by no means sold on it. There were others that appealed to her more. Harwood was quite old and located in a small town not too far from Cleveland. There were only a few more than a thousand students and this seemed rather small to Pam. Why, it wasn't even as large as Glen High! And there were no sororities or fraternities there, only clubs. Pam thought disdainfully that Mike was welcome to go there if he liked, but she had other ideas.

Aloud she said flatly, "It doesn't sound so hot to me."

"Why, Pam?" Penny's voice was troubled.

"Oh, lots of reasons," Pam said.

"It's a good school," Mike argued.

He proceeded to give the reasons for his opinion, with Penny backing him up staunchly. Pam couldn't help wondering, her glance going from Mike to Penny and back again, whether there was a suggestion of pressure being brought to bear upon her. Probably, she realized resentfully, the two of them had already hatched a full-scale plot to attend the same college. But if they imagined they could manipulate her into any such course, they were badly mistaken! She meant to pick her own school, and not strictly according to Mike Bradley's ideas, either! If Penny had her heart set on trailing after him, it was just too bad. They'd both find that out.

As the enthusiastic discussion of Harwood College and its many merits went on, Pam felt a stubbornness of which she hadn't known she was capable rising within her.

5   *A Difference of Opinion*

A FEW nights later Pam came out of her bed-room after dressing for a date with Randy to find Penny and Mike ensconced on the couch, dark head and fair almost touching as they pored over a Harwood College catalogue. Their voices broke over her like a tide, telling her what a wonderful school Harwood was. And nothing would do but that Pam must sit down and look at the catalogue with them, although she explained that she had only a few minutes before Randy would be along. They got Mother in on the discussion, too, and she lis-tened with obvious interest and approval to all the things Mike and Penny told about Harwood. The good student-teacher ratio. The well-known people who were alumni of the school. The location, which, Make explained drily, was far enough away from home for independence, but not so far that trips back for the holidays would break you.

"Doesn't it sound just perfect?" Penny exclaimed, an

eager little note in her voice that Pam had to steel her heart against. "I'd love to go there."

Mother nodded, admitting, "There are a lot of things about it I like very much. What do you think, Pam?"

"It's not something to be decided all in a rush," Pam said coolly. "There are other schools I like better."

"Oh, Pam, why?" Penny coaxed. "It sounds wonderful to me. None of the others we can afford compares with it."

Mother's blue gaze was quietly thoughtful on Pam's face. Pam had the feeling it penetrated too deeply and her own eyes fell under that level, evaluating look. She said, her tone sharply annoyed, "To hear you and Mike go on, you'd think Harwood was the best college in the whole country!"

Before Penny could answer, Mother said, "Of course, it's not wise to hurry such an important decision. You should both be satisfied with whatever school you choose."

"But we've already considered so many," Penny argued. "And if we don't decide pretty soon, we may not be able to get in at all."

Mike tactfully said nothing, but his silence backed her up eloquently.

After a moment, Mother asked, "There isn't anything special you don't like about Harwood, is there, Pam?"

Nothing, Pam thought, except that Mike's so sold on it. And I'm not going to let him order my life, just because Penny thinks she can't live without him. Why does she want to go to the same school he's chosen, any-way? It's quite silly the way she gives in to all his wishes, as if she didn't have a mind of her own at all!

She looked up at Mother, her gray glance stormy with all the churning feelings she was trying so hard to keep beneath the surface. "Oh, nothing special, I suppose," she admitted shortly. "It's just that I can't see why Penny's so keen on it."

Pam noticed how Penny's eyes met Mike's in a long look. Do something, Mike, Penny's glance said clearly. Help me persuade her.

Mike said, his grin ingratiating, "Don't be like that, Pam. You know how much Pen and I want to go to the same college. And Harwood sounds best of all the ones we've considered."

"To you, maybe," Pam said.

Mike's eyes met hers squarely and there was a challenging gleam in them. "Why are you so stubborn all of a sudden?" he demanded. "Don't you want Penny and me to go to the same school? Your Mother thinks its okay. Don't you, Mrs. Howard?"

"I see no reason why you shouldn't," Mother said.

"It's silly to think I care about that," Pam told him.

"Then it must be that you don't want to go to the same college with me," Mike pressed bluntly. "Why, Pam?"

"That's silly, too," Pam said, feeling her heart beat faster, pumping the blood through her veins at a dizzy pace. She thought, This must be what a lie-detecting machine picks up and shows on a chart as a lot of pointed zig-zags.

But luckily there was no lie detector, nothing to give her away. And aloud she added merely, "Must you take everything from such a personal angle, Mike? Just because

I'm not sold on Harwood doesn't mean I've got anything against you."

She heard the downstairs door-bell ring then and knew that it must be Randy. Never had an interruption been more welcome, never had she murmured a hasty good-bye and hurried down to meet him with more genuine delight. Opening the door, she slipped out into the summer night and almost into Randy's surprised arms.

"Wonders will never cease," he said drily. "You're ready."

"If you start picking on me now, too," Pam said, as they went down the walk, "I can't take it. Enough is enough!"

Randy helped her into the green convertible, then went around and got in beside her. As they rolled away from the curb, he asked, "Who's been picking on you?"

"Oh, not picking exactly," Pam admitted, leaning back and letting the summer wind ruffle her hair with cool fingers. "But Penny and Mike are working so hard on me about that darned college and I can't see what's so special about it."

"Harwood, you mean? It sounds pretty good to me."

Pam shrugged. "No better than several others."

"But unless you've got a particular school in mind that you prefer to it," Randy argued, "I should think you could be big about the situation and let Penny have her way."

"Mike, you mean," Pam said and felt once more the quick hot pulsing of anger. "It makes me so mad the way Penny just leaps to do whatever Mike wants her to!"

"Aw, you imagine that," Randy said good-naturedly. "Sure, they're pretty fond of each other. But it works both ways. Mike would want just as much to please Penny as vice versa. The thing is, they're so keen on going to the same school and if this one seems to offer what they want—"

He left it at that. Pam's jaw set stubbornly.

She asked, "Can't we talk about anything else? I'm sick of the whole business."

But for once Randy didn't immediately accede to her wishes. He said slowly, "You know what I sometimes wonder?"

Pam shook her head.

"Whether you aren't kind of jealous of Mike."

"Of all the ridiculous things to say!" Pam gasped.

"I mean jealous of his influence on Penny," Randy pursued his train of thought doggedly. "She used to turn to you so much for advice, she used to sort of copy you. I've heard her admit it herself. But now she's more independent, more her own self. And maybe, unconsciously, you resent her slipping out from under your influence. Maybe you blame Mike for it when actually it's just that Penny's becoming more mature."

"Really," Pam said icily, "that is the most fantastic bit of nonsense I've ever heard. What do you think you are, a psychoanalyst or something?"

"I was figuring on investing in a second-hand couch," Randy grinned, "and going into business."

"Save your money," Pam advised. "You're a failure already."

"I'm not so sure of that," Randy argued. "I've even got another theory that might account for your behavior."

"Do tell me, Dr. Kirkpatrick," Pam cooed. "I can't wait

to hear your newest interpretation of my subconscious."

"It could be," Randy said, after a moment's stretching silence, "that you're jealous of Penny."

"Jealous of Penny?" Pam repeated incredulously. "Why?"

"Because Mike's so crazy about her," Randy said.

"And why should I be jealous because of that?" With an effort Pam kept her tone even.

"Maybe jealous isn't the right word," Randy said. "Maybe 'resentful' would be better. Maybe you resent Penny's taking Mike over and his being so important to her. Could it all be tied up with the complication of you and Penny being twins, I wonder?"

"Or could you just be off your rocker?" Pam suggested.

"That's a possibility, too," Randy admitted, chuckling.

Pam laughed, too. It was better to laugh, she felt, than to grow angry, although hot, unreasonable rage out of all proportion to the cause bubbled like lava just under the surface of her apparent amusement.

Randy had no right to talk that way to her, to put such ugly ideas into her mind, even though he was half-kidding. Or was he serious, she wondered? Did he actually think that jealousy and resentment toward her sister and Mike were at the core of her unwillingness to give in to their wishes about college? But that was absurd, Pam told herself. She loved Penny, she wouldn't willingly do anything to make her unhappy. And certainly she cherished no hard feelings against Mike, although losing him to Penny had been something of a blow to her ego. But she had gotten over that long ago. And the mere fact that Mike still was attractive to her surely couldn't affect her whole pattern of behavior toward him and Penny, as Randy's silly explanation of her conduct would imply.

"If anyone asks me for a reference," Pam said aloud, "I'll tell them you're a big fake."

"Heck," Randy said, "there's my fascinating career in psychoanalysis nipped in the bud." After a moment he asked, "But if I'm all wrong about it, just why don't you want to go to Harwood College when Penny and Mike are so keen on it?"

Pam sighed. "Can't we drop the subject? I'm tired of discussing it."

"I guess we'll have to," Randy said. "Here's the drive-in."

A good movie unrolling before your eyes is a wonderful cure for too much thinking, Pam found. She quite succeeded in losing herself in the imaginary troubles besetting the heroine of the film. She even managed to evade the tiny voice within her which sought to argue that there might be a grain of truth in Randy's version of her motives. By the time the show was over Pam's anger with Randy and her distrust of herself were alike entirely dissipated.

They didn't get back to the subject of college at all. Randy drove out along the river road and they stopped at a little restaurant for sodas. And then, because the night was fine and it wasn't very late, they drove on a bit further, and Randy stopped the car at a point where there was little traffic and only the murmur of frogs and crickets and the gentle lapping sound of water to disturb the dark stillness.

He drew Pam into his arms and their lips met and clung for a moment. His kiss wasn't distasteful to Pam, but it didn't stir her. It was just Randy's kiss, familiar, to be taken for granted, nothing to get very excited about. But she could feel the quickened beat of his heart and knew that the kiss wasn't, for him, such a casual matter.

Randy said, his voice husky, "Gee, Pam, I'm going to miss you when I go East. I wish you could come, too."

Pam didn't wish it at all. She was looking forward to the chance college would afford for her to substitute someone more exciting for Randy. Not that she didn't like him well enough. But certainly there was nothing serious in her feelings toward him, nothing worth prolonging.

She said, not wanting him to know how she felt lest their pleasant easy relationship fail to last out the summer, "We'll always be friends, Randy. I'm very fond of you. You know that." Even in her own ears the words sounded flat and insipid.

"Fond is a piddling little word for the way I feel about you," Randy told her. "Is friends all we'll ever be, Pam?"

"We're too young to get serious—" Pam began.

But Randy broke in almost roughly, "I don't feel too young, Pam. I'm in love with you."

"Oh, Randy," Pam said, her voice distressed. "Don't spoil things."

After a moment Randy asked, "Is that what my loving you would do, spoil things?"

"I'm not ready to fall in love," Pam said. "Not with you, not with anyone. I'm not sure enough of myself yet, not sure what I want, what would make me happy. You should feel the same way."

"Maybe I already know what I want," Randy's tone was wry.

"Oh, Randy," Pam said gently, "you just think that. You'll meet so many other girls when you're away at college, you'll forget all about me."

"Oh, sure!" Randy said, his voice harsh. "Is that what you're figuring on doing, forgetting me?"

Pam tried to keep her impatience from sounding through her tone. "I don't see why you want to make such an issue of everything lately," she told him. "Why must you get so serious?"

After a moment Randy asked, not too steadily, his belligerence gone, "Would you—rather not date me anymore, Pam? Maybe that's the best solution. Because I seem to have lost my light touch where you're concerned."

"Of course not," Pam denied quickly. That wasn't what she wanted at all. She said in her most wistful, coaxing way, "Can't we just let things ride as they have been? Please, Randy?"

Her voice stopped and there was no sound in the night except the croaking of frogs and the sprightly chatter of crickets and the murmur of the water. Randy sat staring straight ahead, his profile strained and unhappy in the moonlight. It hurt Pam to see him so. Impulsively she reached out to lay her hand on his.

Randy turned his hand over and gave her fingers a tight reassuring squeeze. He even managed a grin, although it was a somewhat feeble effort. "Yeah," he sighed. "Yeah, I guess so."

But the night and the place and being together seemed to have lost their magic. Randy turned the ignition switch and the convertible's motor roared into life.

6   The Double Cross

Some decision about college would have to be reached soon. Time was running out. Penny, Pam knew, was just as conscious of this as she was. Yet the question of whether or not they should attend Harwood lay dormant. Pam felt that Penny was purposely evading the issue, giving her time to get used to the idea of Harwood, so that the sharp edges of her resistance might wear down.

Using psychology on me, Pam thought drily. But it won't help.

The thought of psychology summoned up a disturbing memory. Not even to herself would Pam admit that there might have been some truth in Randy's analysis of her motives. Jealous of Mike? Resentful of Penny? How absurd could you get? She was simply, she told herself, declining to let Mike Bradley make up her mind for her.

Once when she and Mother happened to be alone in the shop during a brief lull between customers, Pam asked her, "Do you think it's a good idea for Penny and Mike to go to the same college? He seems to have such a strong influence on her."

A little smile tugged at the corner of Mother's mouth as she looked up from a new bolt of drapery material she had been examining. "Do you think it's a bad influence, Pam?" she asked, her tone only half serious.

"No," Pam had to admit in all honesty. "But you felt it was such a fine thing when Penny learned to make her own decisions and not depend so much on me. So I should think the same thing would hold true in her relationship with Mike."

Mother said, more soberly now as she saw how earnest Pam was, "I'm not worried about Penny that way any longer. She's become a lot more adult in the past year. And Mike's 'influence' on her, as you call it—well, I don't think it's any stronger than her influence on him. They mean so much to each other—"

"But that's just it," Pam broke in. "Don't you think it would be better for Penny to meet different boys, not just cling to Mike, as she's bound to do if they go to the same school?"

Celia Howard thought about that for a moment, then she said, "Penny will meet different boys at college, whether Mike's there or not. And I think she's mature enough to judge whether Mike is more important to her than the others. Mike and Penny are both so sensible. They'll work things out."

Pam had the impression that her mother meant to go on and say something more, but some customers came in just then and the opportunity was lost.

Did Mother feel, Pam wondered, that she was less mature and sensible than Penny? Resentment flared up in her at the mere suspicion. Just because Penny had gained some measure of poise and self-confidence, just because she had begun making up her own mind instead of basing her decisions on Pam's judgments—well, that certainly didn't detract any from her, Pam's, poise and self-confidence. And she had been making her own decisions for years.

It seemed to her, trying to find a peg on which to hang all her smouldering dissatisfactions and resentments, that Mike Bradley was the cause of most of her problems. Before she and Penny had met him, things had been much smoother and simpler. Darn Mike anyway, Pam thought with quiet in-turned rage.

A few nights later Pam was handed a perfect opportunity for working off some of her annoyance with Mike. And it all came about without a bit of connivance on her part—up to a certain point, that was.

Often, when Mike was working and Pam didn't happen to have a date, she and Penny would go to the movies. Mike would be ushering, or taking tickets during the early part of the evening, but when the last show was well under way, he would be free to join the girls and walk home with them. Such had been their plan on this particular night, but Penny developed a headache at dinner time and decided that watching a double feature would only make it worse. It was too late to call Mike and tell him of her change of plan; besides, one of the films was a musical Pam had especially been looking forward to seeing.

"Why don't you go anyway?" Penny suggested. "Then you can tell Mike I had a headache and he'll walk you home."

"I suppose I could do that," Pam agreed, "if you wouldn't mind"

Penny said, "Of course I don't. All I'm going to do is get to bed early. No use to spoil your evening, too."

So Pam proceeded to dress in her yellow peasant skirt and a ruffly, feminine blouse. And merely because Penny's short fleece coat was hanging in the closet where it belonged and her own had been tossed aside in some momentarily unremembered spot, she wore Penny's. The casual switch meant nothing, certainly there was no ulterior motive involved. The two girls so often wore each other's clothes that whether she put on Penny's coral-colored coat or her own green one had slight significance. Pam didn't give the matter a conscious thought.

It wasn't until she had reached the theater and bought her ticket and had gone inside that she began to realize that the groundwork had been inadvertently laid for a natural mistake. She encountered Mike in the dim inner lobby and, as he led her down the darkened aisle to a seat, he murmured, "What happened to Pam?"

To—Pam? Almost, but not quite, Pam repeated his words aloud. Then it struck her that this was too good a joke to spoil. Mike, taking her for Penny—nothing like that had happened in such a long while! And Pam used to love fooling people, confusing them as to just which twin they were talking to, if there seemed to be even the slightest trace of uncertainty in their minds.

She managed to curb the amusement bubbling up within her as she whispered back, "She had a headache."

"Oh," Mike said, "too bad."

Pam nodded solicitously and Mike murmured, "See you later," and went on back to his station at the end of the aisle.

All during the show, to which she gave only the

surface layer of her mind, Pam savored the richness of the joke she meant to play on Mike. Since he had taken her for Penny, Pam saw no reason for enlightening him. It should be easy enough to continue the harmless deception, provided she was careful to avoid any place where the lights might be too mercilessly revealing.

I wonder, Pam thought, what Penny and Mike talk about when they're alone? I wonder if they ever discuss me—and what they say?

It would be interesting and informative to find out, she reflected. Of course, if Mike had realized his mistake by the time he joined her, she could always pretend she had thought his inquiry had been about "Pen" instead of "Pam." It would be a quite natural mistake on her part and nothing to be embarrassed over.

But when Mike slipped into the empty seat beside her more than an hour later he was still obviously laboring under the delusion that she was Penny. He didn't have to say a word for Pam to realize that. The way he reached over to take her hand warmly and strongly in his was a sufficient indication of his error.

With an exultant little smile, Pam curled her fingers in his, just as she had seen Penny do so often. And when the show was over and they went out into the lobby, still hand in hand, Pam quickened her pace just enough to keep a bit ahead so that he couldn't get a full view of her face.

Mike pulled her to a slower pace as they reached the safer dimness of the street. "What's your mad rush?" he asked good-humoredly.

"Oh, was I going too fast?" Pam murmured innocently.

"I might have bought you a candy bar if you hadn't

gone through the lobby in such a hurry," he told her.

Pam shook her head. "Bad for the complexion," she offered the same excuse she'd often heard Penny use in declining. "Thanks just the same, though."

Mike's fingers stayed locked with hers as they strolled slowly down the street. Pam felt her heart race and a kind of warmth flow through her that was never engendered by Randy's touch. When should she tell Mike the truth? When should she make him feel foolish for getting Penny and her confused? Not yet, a small inner voice whispered, not too steadily. Not quite yet. It would be such delicious fun to continue the masquerade just a bit longer.

"Like a soda?" Mike asked, as they approached the drugstore.

Pam said, hoping her momentary panic didn't sound through her voice, "Oh, I don't think so, Mike. Let's— let's just go for a walk, shall we?"

"Through the park," Mike agreed, squeezing her fingers.

The park lay dim and quiet in the moonlight. Pam and Mike took the graveled walk that led along one shore of the small lake. They talked and were companionably silent and talked again. Pam was careful to avoid her usual vivacious chatter, lest Mike sense his mistake.

Once Mike asked, "Any luck yet persuading Pam to go to Harwood?"

Pam said slowly, speaking just as Penny would have spoken, she felt sure, "I've been sort of letting things rest, hoping she'd be more willing if we gave her time to get used to the idea."

"Yeah," Mike said, "let's keep our fingers crossed. She sure is stubborn about it."

Pam said, knowing her sister's loyalty, "But she has a right to choose the college she wants, Mike. We can't expect her just to go overboard for Harwood if she isn't sure."

Mike pulled Pam close into the circle of his arm and pressed his cheek against her hair. "There you go again," he said, his tone gently teasing, "making excuses for her. Sure, she has a right to choose, but so do you. And you'd think, for once, she could put your preference ahead of her own, when she knows how much it means to both of us."

Of all the positions for a girl to be in, Pam thought, amusement and resentment, with just an undercurrent of shame, warring within her. Standing there, pretending to be Penny, with Mike's arm around her, while he condemned her, Pam's, actions! She wanted to laugh, but in some twisted crazy way, she felt like crying, too.

But, of course, she could do neither. So she merely said, her voice coaxing, "Let's not talk about it now, Mike."

And so they walked on as before, sometimes speaking and sometimes silent. And when they had traversed the length of the little park, their footsteps led them along familiar streets toward Howard House. Only the inner hall light had been left burning against Pam's return. But she couldn't risk even that illumination. Because sometime during the evening, Pam wasn't quite sure when, she had lost all urge to confess her deception to Mike, to laugh at his discomfiture. Why, she asked herself, had she got into such a spot? And how could she escape without letting Mike know the truth?

As he followed her across the deeper darkness of the little entrance porch, Pam felt panic mounting within her.

"Can't I come in for a minute?" Mike asked, as she stood hesitant at the door. "It's not much after ten."

"But you have to get up so early," Pam objected.

"Such solicitude," Mike chuckled.

"I have to get up early, too," Pam admitted. "Tomorrow's my day to work. And we've got a shipment of furniture coming in we'll have to make room for. I think you'd better go, Mike."

Maybe Penny wouldn't have been so adamant, Pam realized. But she couldn't take a chance of Mike recognizing her.

"Okay, okay," Mike said. "You've convinced me."

But he took a step closer and Pam was in his arms and his face, dim in the darkness, was coming down to hers. She could feel the beat of his heart against her and she found herself wanting, more than she could ever remember having wanted anything in her life, to feel his lips on hers.

Tell him, her conscience said clearly, sternly. Tell him now that you're Pam, not Penny.

But Pam ignored the voice, her hands tight on Mike's shoulders, her lips lifting to his. As he kissed her, she felt her own heart quicken and the magic of the night, the moment, washed over her in slow waves. Then, as the kiss ended, Pam drew a deep, shaken breath and pulled away from Mike, opening the door and slipping inside with only a choked, "Good-night."

She leaned there, just inside, against the door she had shut behind her. And for a moment she didn't think at all, but only felt the warm, uplifting aftermath of that stolen caress. It was the faint sound of Mike's footsteps, going rather slowly away, that brought her back to the present and a quick upsurge of shame for what she had done . . .

7 *The Quarrel*

PAM was glad she was busy the next day, almost too busy to think, to face squarely the deep sense of shame that rose in her whenever she remembered the previous evening. How could she have done such a thing to Penny, who trusted her? That was the question that formed in her troubled mind again and again. She tried to keep her attention fixed on drapery material and lounge chairs and stark white modern lamps, on all the familiar details that were a part of helping Mother in the shop. But her mind wandered despite her efforts to keep it focused on the business at hand. And she would feel again the touch of Mike's fingers and know once more the stolen magic of his kiss there in the summer darkness. And then she would think of Penny and shame would well up in her.

Near lunch-time Gran dropped in, bringing a pan of warm, newly baked pecan rolls. Lucius, she said, had gone in to the city for the day on business.

"He invited me to go along," Gran said, "but I hate Chicago on a hot sticky day. Only trouble is, I hate eating alone, too. So I figured if I brought you some rolls you'd ask me to stay to lunch."

"And so we will," Mother informed her, laughing. "You didn't even have to bring the rolls. Come on upstairs. Penny must have lunch about ready."

There was usually a noontime lull in business at Howard House. So they trooped upstairs and found that Penny had salad and tall glasses of iced tea already on the table. She had slept away her headache of the night before and she looked fresh and pretty in a yellow sun-dress that left her tanned back bare. She greeted Gran with pleasure and laid an extra place on the gay cloth and poured another glass of tea.

When they were seated around the table, Gran said conversationally, her smiling glance on Penny, "Lucius and I saw you at the show last night. But you and Mike rushed across the lobby so fast, we couldn't catch up with you. We were going to offer you a lift home, but the way you were holding hands, it looked like you'd rather be alone, anyway."

In the moment of silence that followed, Pam felt Penny's eyes and Mother's staring at her. A hot embarrassed flush rose to her cheeks. She tried to say something, but no words obeyed her brain's command. What could she say?

After a brief pause, Penny told Gran simply, "I wasn't there. It was Pam you saw." There was a note of tension in her voice that Gran was quick to detect.

"But I was sure—" she began. And stopped. Because what could Gran say, either?

Pam had herself under better control now, the first

shock was past and her mind was working lucidly. She even managed a little laugh as she asked Gran, "Wasn't it a riot? He took me for Penny and I got such a bang out of Mike—of all people!—making a mistake like that, I just couldn't enlighten him right away. You know, Pen," her glance sought her sister's now, "how I always used to enjoy fooling people. And no one's got us mixed up in such a long time! I simply had to string Mike along for awhile."

When her gay voice stopped, there was uneasy silence.

Then Gran said ruefully, "I guess I spilled the beans."

Mother's tone was grave, her blue glance direct on Pam's face as she asked, "Didn't you mean to tell Penny, Pam? It seems like quite a shabby trick to me."

"Oh, for creep's sake!" Pam cried impatiently. "Why do you all act as though I'd done something perfectly horrible? It was just a joke. Of course, I meant to tell Penny and Mike, too."

Almost, under the censure in Gran's and Mother's eyes, the stark accusation in Penny's, Pam could believe that what she said was true. She would have told Penny eventually, she assured herself hotly. It was silly of them to imagine she wouldn't. And as for Mike Bradley, it served him right. If a boy couldn't tell his own girl from her sister—

Her thought broke as Penny asked flatly, "But you didn't tell Mike last night? You let him go through the whole evening thinking you were me?"

For a wild instant Pam felt an impulse to lie, to tell Penny that she had enlightened Mike before the evening was over. If she could warn Mike before he talked with

Penny, he might even back her up, since he, too, must see that Penny would be less hurt by a lie than the truth. But Pam's temptation died quickly. She couldn't lie to Penny. They were too close, they knew each other too well. Penny would see through her, just as she would see through any pretense on Mike's part. The truth would be best.

"No," Pam admitted, "I didn't tell him—yet."

Penny said nothing more. Her eyes dropped from Pam's and she began eating. Gran and Mother took their cue from her and followed suit. The conversation, rather stilted at first but growing more easy, drifted to other topics. Pam tried to take part in it with her usual animation, tried not to notice how quiet Penny was. But unease grew in her and the realization that Penny would undoubtedly have some questions to ask when they were alone lay like a weight upon her. And Mother would take her to task, too, and Mike would be furious when he found out the truth. But more than anything else, it was the sense of her own wrong-doing that took the edge off Pam's appetite and made her toy with her salad and eat one of Gran's delicious pecan rolls without even tasting it.

When lunch was over, Gran offered to help Mother in the shop for awhile. Pam knew it was a ruse to leave her and Penny alone together, to give them a chance to talk out their difficulties. Apprehension made her jittery as the two older women went downstairs. Then the phone rang, affording Pam a temporary reprieve. She was glad when Penny went to answer it.

But her heart gave a queer twist as she heard her twin say, "Hello? . . . Oh, hello, Mike . . ."

That does it, Pam thought. Now she'll tell him and—oh, darn it, why didn't I have sense enough not to get myself into all this?

She proceeded to clear the table and stack the dishes rather noisily in the sink. The rush of water from the faucet also helped her keep from listening to Penny's part of the telephone conversation. Pam tried not to think, as well as not to hear, but the clatter of dishes and silver, the sound of running water, weren't so effective in stopping her thoughts. She had the dishes half done when Penny came out to the kitchen.

"That was Mike," Penny said, an angry crispness in her voice. "You didn't have him as completely fooled as you thought."

Pam's questioning glance came up to meet hers and Penny went on, "He told me to tell you he did take you for me at the show and even walking home. But when you kissed him good-night, he knew the difference."

Pam felt rage and humiliation redden her face. She glared back at Penny, exclaiming, "That would be easy enough for him to say when he knew you'd found out about it!"

But Penny shook her head. "You're wrong. He did know. The first thing he said just now was, 'Did Pam tell you what she did last night?' That was before I'd told him about Gran seeing you, or anything. He knew, all right. And he's awfully mad at you. And so am I," Penny said, her gray eyes glinting furiously. "I think it was a low, sneaky trick you pulled! You know how Mike and I feel about each other. What were you trying to do?"

Pam's voice rose. "It was just a joke and you act as if it

was something terrible! I only wanted to fool Mike—I'd have told you—"

"Would you, Pam?" Penny asked sternly. "If it hadn't been for the accident of what Gran said, I wonder if you wouldn't just have kept quiet, waiting to see whether Mike had caught on or not. And if he hadn't, I doubt I'd ever have learned what you did. I think you'd have kept it all locked up inside of you, a kind of cruel secret to gloat over."

"What an awful way to talk to me," Pam gulped, tears pressing hard against her eyelids. "You've changed so, Penny, since you've fallen for Mike Bradley. You'd never have accused me of such things before."

Penny said, "Maybe I never saw through you before! How could you do such a thing behind my back?"

"I told you it was just a joke," Pam choked. "We used to fool people sometimes and you never took it so hard."

"But that wasn't the same," Penny argued. "Can't you see it wasn't? We were children then, now we're grown up." She accused Pam, "You kissed Mike and you had no right to—it was like stealing—" her voice ran down and she stared at her sister, eyes wide and starkly questioning. "It doesn't make sense," she said then, her tone shocked, "unless you're still attracted to Mike—unless you want him for yourself and are jealous of me—"

Pam had to stop her. She couldn't have Penny probing into her feelings like that, bringing out into the open things she had tried to keep hidden even from herself. She felt the hot tears spill over and run down her cheeks as she sobbed, "You haven't any right to talk that way—to accuse me—" She broke off and ran out of the kitchen and into the bedroom, slamming the door behind her . . .

Pam lay there on her bed, muffling the sounds of her wild weeping with her pillow. Emotions struggled against each other within her. At first anger and resentment toward Penny were the strongest, but gradually these were overcome by a kind of sick shame at her own inexcusable conduct. It was never easy for Pam to see, or at least to admit, that she was wholly in the wrong. She could always find such logical excuses for her conduct. But now, search as she might, she was without defenses against the accusations of her own conscience.

She seemed to hear again Penny's hurt voice saying, "You had no right to kiss Mike—it was like stealing—"

And in her heart Pam knew that her sister's words were true. Under other circumstances, it might have been different. Had Mike known who she was, had he kissed her of his own volition, the situation would not have been the same. But she had tricked him, she had stolen that caress which had climaxed a stolen evening. She had pretended to be Penny and Mike had been deceived until he kissed her.

What was so special about Penny's kiss, Pam asked herself rebelliously?

And a small voice within her answered, Penny loves Mike, while you simply want to win him back to prove to yourself you can. When he was yours for the taking, you liked him no better than Randy and the others. It was his being attracted to Penny that enhanced his value in your eyes.

Pam lay there, her face hot in the damp pillow, hearing and yet not hearing the everyday sounds of a summer afternoon going on outside the window. The cars passing by. The voices of children. The intermittent song of birds in the tall old trees that shaded Howard House. But try as she would to shut her ears to it, the voice inside her was louder than these familiar sounds.

It said in detached accusation, Randy was partly right, you know. Randy saw through you, which was why you resented what he said. You have been jealous of your own sister for winning Mike away. And you've fought against his influence on her, not for her sake, but because you liked having her cling to you and take your advice and seek your help in making decisions. That built you up and made you feel important. But Penny has become more mature than you, for all your poise and assurance. In deep, vital ways, Penny is more grown up. And you don't like it, you can scarcely bring yourself to face the fact. So you look around for someone to blame for your own shortcomings and Mike's your scapegoat. That's why you've fought against going to the college of his and Penny's choice. You've wanted to separate them.

The noises outside the window went on. Pam's thoughts continued to sit as judge and jury on her recent actions. She wasn't crying now, she was past tears. Still, she couldn't lift her face from the shelter of the pillow.

After awhile she was aware that the door had opened and closed. Then the bedsprings gave a little as someone sat down beside her. Still Pam didn't raise her head. She felt a hand on her shoulder and knew that it was Mother's hand, even before Celia spoke, before she said gently, "Don't cry any more, Pam."

"I'm not," Pam said. "I'm just—so ashamed, I don't know what to do."

Mother's hand stroked her shoulder. "I know."

Pam said, her voice still muffled by the pillow, "I don't see why Penny should ever forgive me—but I can't bear it if she won't. I don't see how I could have acted the way I did."

"She'll forgive you," Mother said, "if you're sorry. Wouldn't you forgive her if she'd done something that hurt you and then saw she was in the wrong and felt ashamed?"

Pam said in a small, choked voice, "Penny wouldn't pull a low trick like that. She's got too much sense. She doesn't do crazy things on impulse—and then wish she could just die."

Mother comforted, "Everyone does things they're ashamed of sometimes. Penny's mature enough to realize that."

"She's more mature than I am," Pam admitted. And as though that confession had opened the floodgates, she found herself spilling out to Mother all the things she had only so recently acknowledged to herself. Telling her what Randy had said and how she had come to realize the truth of it. Putting into hesitant words the ugly fact that she had been holding out against the school both Penny and Mike wanted to attend, just to be contrary, to make things hard for Mike.

"But if you see these things now," Mother said, "you can do something about them. It's only when we're too blind to realize the causes of our own bad actions that we have to worry. Penny will see that. She'll forgive you, I know."

"Maybe," Pam's tone was still doubtful, "if I tell her what a dope I've been, if I give in about Harwood—" her hopeful glance went to Mother's face as she lifted her head at last. "Oh, Mother, do you think she'll ever trust me again?"

Celia nodded. "Ask her. I don't believe Penny or Mike, either, will hold out against you, now that you're able to see you've been in the wrong."

8 *What About Randy?*

MAKING up with Penny was easier than Pam had dared to hope. She should have realized that the close bond between them would tend to make her twin just as miserable over any threatened serious break as she herself was. Besides, Pam's abject apology, her unqualified admission that she was wholly in the wrong, were so unprecedented Penny was bound to be touched.

Before the pinkness caused by Pam's tears had faded from her eyelids, Penny had forgiven her. And when Pam went on to capitulate completely on the long-unsettled question of college, any resentment that might still have lingered in Penny's heart was quenched by the flood of her delight and relief.

"Oh, Pam!" she exclaimed, her own eyes suspiciously bright and her voice a bit unsteady with emotion. "You really mean it? You'll go to Harwood?"

Pam nodded, admitting ruefully, "I guess the only

reason I've been such a louse about it was because I unconsciously wanted to make things tough for Mike. And I knew I was hurting you, too, but I couldn't seem to stop anyway. Oh, Penny, how can a person get into such a state? I'm glad it's all come out into the open at last, so I can get it off my mind."

"So am I," Penny said. "It's seemed lately as if there were a sort of wall, shutting us apart, so that we couldn't talk things out the way we always have, so that I couldn't reach you."

"I felt that way, too," Pam agreed. "Only I didn't blame myself for putting up the wall, I figured it was Mike who had come between us. So I hit back at him every way I could, like holding out against Harwood—and then last night, fooling him and trying to make him feel silly—" her voice trailed off.

Penny's gray glance was direct, almost too direct on Pam's. She asked, "Do you—still like Mike, Pam? I mean a lot—the way you used to before he and I began going together?"

Pam's eyes didn't fall before her sister's. She felt the old temptation to cover up, to seek to hide the truth even from herself, but with an effort she resisted it. She said, her voice low, "I'm not quite sure. For awhile I felt I was attracted to him, more than to Randy or Joe or any of the others. But I wonder if it isn't just that he hasn't been paying any attention to me and the others have. You know how I am, Pen," she said, a little rueful grin tugging at the corner of her mouth. "I can't seem to help it, either. If I've got a boy all sewed up, then I begin to lose interest. If he's hard to get, that makes him practically irresistible."

Penny said flatly, "Well, just remember, hands off Mike." There was a laughing glint in her eye that lightened the solemnity of her tone, but Pam knew she wasn't entirely kidding.

"Okay," Pam agreed meekly. "After last night, I know it's hopeless anyway."

In a way Pam was glad the quarrel between her and Penny had occurred, although she would always feel a qualm of humiliation over the circumstances that had brought it about. But afterward, their relationship seemed to settle back onto its old firm foundation. No longer was there the friction, the pulling two ways that seemed to have existed between them over college and Mike Bradley. They were twins again in the fullest, richest sense of the word, knowing a special closeness and understanding because of the accident of simultaneous birth.

Pam enjoyed, too, being back in Mike's good graces, as she was after the first natural upsurge of his anger against her had cooled and he had learned that she had given in on the question of college.

"So you finally decided to stop being a stinker," he said in his old kidding, half-brotherly way.

"If you go calling me names, I might change my mind again," Pam threatened.

"I take it back," Mike said in mocking abject apology.

His hand caught Penny's then and he swung her into a gay jitter-bug step around the Howards' living-room. Pam hadn't seen them both so crazily care-free and happy in a long time. They danced till they fell in a laughing state of exhaustion on the couch beside Pam. And Mike reached out to put an arm around each girl and give them a bear hug.

"Boy!" Mike said feelingly. "Will we have fun at Harwood, the three of us."

"All right," Pam said, "convince me. What's going to be so wonderful about Harwood?"

Listening to Penny and Mike wax enthusiastic, Pam felt a new sense of anticipation rising within her. It was as though she had kept her own expectations dammed up by her perverse decision not to go to the college of Mike's and Penny's choice. Now, listening with an open mind, she found herself catching fire from their enthusiasm and realized that the school really did have a lot to offer.

"They have a fine dramatics department," Penny told her. "You've always been interested in that sort of thing."

Pam knew that Penny had mentioned this fact before, but it had made little or no impression on her then. Now she found herself warming with excitement at the idea of studying dramatics.

"They even have a showboat they operate in the summer," Mike put in. "It goes up and down the river with a student crew, giving old-fashioned melodramas in different towns where they tie up."

Pam stared at him in surprise. "You mean it? I didn't see anything about that in their literature."

Still, she realized, she hadn't looked at the catalogue very thoroughly. She had been so bent and determined not to go to Harwood, she hadn't paid much attention to it.

"But that's a summer course," Penny put in. "We couldn't be gone in the summer, too, Pam. Mother couldn't afford it and anyway we wouldn't want to leave her all alone."

"Oh," Pam remembered, with a little pinch of disappointment. "That's right."

Still they went on discussing the college showboat, just because it was unique and so interesting. And even if she couldn't enroll in the unusual course, because it wouldn't be fair to Mother, Pam found her imagination dwelling on it. A real honest-to-goodness showboat, like the ones that used to ply the rivers when girls wore hoopskirts and movies hadn't even been invented. And a student crew that, in addition to putting on the plays, had to set scenes and supply music, handle the lighting and costumes, sell tickets and swab decks. It sounded quite fabulous and Pam felt a surge of regret over her and Penny's inability to participate in it. Still, she tried to cheer herself, a college that was original enough to offer such a course must make a lot of other advantages available to its students. And in those she and Penny could take part.

Pam realized with a little inner start that Mike's arm was still around her shoulders, just as his other one was around Penny's. But it was such a brotherly gesture, she was able to enjoy the casual camaraderie it signified. Was this a start toward getting over her secret fancy for Mike, Pam wondered. Maybe, if she worked hard at it, he would begin to seem like a brother to her eventually . . .

Pam had a date that night with Randy. They went with Sue Farnsworth and Mitch Martin to the drive-in. Pam had made a point, without being too obvious about it, of not going out with Randy alone since that night when they had parked on the river bank. The evening was fun, not too exciting, just the show and then a stop afterwards for hamburgers and malteds. Pam managed to avoid any prolonged talk after she and Randy had dropped the others off. She said good-night on the doorstep with a quick kiss and gave as an excuse for not lingering that she had to get up early the next morning to help in the shop.

Penny was still awake when Pam reached the bedroom. She was in bed, but when Pam switched on the shaded dresser lamp, Penny threw an arm across her eyes to shut out the sudden brightness. When her eyes had grown accustomed to it, she raised herself on one elbow to ask Pam, "Have fun?"

"Oh, sure," Pam said casually. She was half undressed by that time. "Did you?"

Penny nodded, her eyes shining, a little smile tilting her mouth. "We went over to Mike's and played bridge with his mother and dad for awhile. They're awfully nice and it was quite a game. Then, it was such a lovely night, we walked all the way around the lake coming home. The moon made such a bright path across the water, it almost seemed as if it could hold you up." She laughed softly. "Mike threatened to try it, but I persuaded him not to."

There was no mistaking the rich happiness in her voice. Still Pam asked wonderingly, "And you really and truly enjoyed it? Just playing cards with Mike's parents and then taking a walk?"

Penny nodded. "I enjoyed it," she said and there was an undertone to the words—Pam sought to identify it. Could it be pity? But how absurd for Penny to pity her, who had had an infinitely more enjoyable evening!

Pam said, "We saw a pretty good show at the drive-in. Then we went out to that new place on the highway south of town. The food's good and it's quite expensive—" she broke off, not liking the petty, show-off way she was talking. After a moment she asked, buttoning her pajamas slowly, "Penny, how can you have fun when Mike never has the money to take you anyplace exciting? You just go on doing the same things, taking walks, going to museums and on picnics, maybe once in awhile to a movie. I'd be bored to death with that same old routine."

Penny said quietly, "I could never be bored with Mike. When you're with someone you care for a lot, it's not the places you go, the things you do, that are important. It's just being together, having the chance to talk and really get to know each other." She asked then, her glance direct and questioning on Pam's face, "Don't you like Randy any more, Pam? He's such a swell person and awfully fond of you."

"Of course, I like him," Pam said rather shortly. "I feel exactly the same way about him I always have. It's Randy who's changed. He gets so serious. But I want to keep things on a fun basis, just as we started out."

She proceeded to snap off the light and get into bed. The springs creaked under her as she wiggled around, trying to get settled. But although she shut her eyes tight against the darkness, she knew she wasn't really sleepy.

Out of a stretching silence, Penny said hesitantly, "Just —don't hurt him, Pam. Randy's sort of sensitive."

"I know," Pam agreed and the words came out in a sigh.

She did know. That was why she was on needles and pins lately, trying to sidestep any serious talk with him. She told Penny, "I don't want to hurt him. I like Randy a lot. If we could just go on being friends the rest of the summer, I'd be happy. I think after that the situation would take care of itself. But Randy's got this sudden urge to play for keeps."

"Has he asked you to get engaged?" Penny queried.

"I've managed to avoid giving him the chance so far. But I'm sure that's what he has in mind."

"But—can't you just tell him the truth, Pam? You could be kind about it, but after all, he'll have to know sometime that you don't like him that well."

"If I come right out with it," Pam said frankly, "I'll have to quit dating him. And you know how I love the country club and all the expensive places Randy takes me. Besides, I really like him better than any of the rest of the boys. So what's the harm if I just try to keep things from coming to a head until this summer's over?"

For a moment Penny didn't answer. Then she said gravely, "The only harm might be to Randy. If he realizes you're just keeping him dangling because of the places he takes you—well, I should think that might hurt him more than anything."

"Then how would you handle it?" Pam pressed.

And she wasn't even aware of how absurd it was for her to be asking Penny's advice on such a matter. She, Pam, who had dealt easily with boys from her earliest teens, who had always had a dozen dates to Penny's one. But maybe it wasn't so absurd, after all. There had always been a core of quiet strength in Penny, a seriousness and sense that bespoke character. And the relationship between Pam and Randy—well, Pam would be the first to admit that it had got rather out of hand, for all her adeptness. It had gone beyond the realm of easy flirtation, of teasing and laughter, where Pam had meant to keep it. Now it had become, at least from Randy's angle, some-

thing more than just the casual girl-and-boy game that
Pam had played with so many others. Depths had developed beneath the surface sparkle and triviality. And it
might be, in such a situation, that Penny could give Pam
advice, instead of the other way around, as it had always
been.

"Well," Penny said thoughtfully, "I wouldn't just
evade the issue. That doesn't settle anything."

"But how can I come right out and tell him the truth?"
Pam demanded. "That would hurt him for sure. And it
would hurt him, too, if I stopped dating him entirely."

Still, she remembered that Randy himself had suggested that possibility the night of their last serious talk.
But she hadn't liked the idea then any more than she did
now.

"I'm not so sure," Penny said stubbornly. "If he's going
to be hurt, it seems to me it had better be by honesty than
deceit. But, of course," she added, "it's your own affair."

Which was true enough. But even though they left it
at that Pam couldn't help wondering whether her sister
might be right . . .

9

A Pair of Loveseats

THE weeks that followed were busy ones for the twins. There were all the details of college enrollment to be taken care of, grade transcripts to have sent off from high school, applications to be filled out, living quarters at the school to be arranged for. Since Glen High was fully accredited, no entrance exams were required, although there would be placement tests at the beginning of the fall term.

As each matter was settled, college seemed to loom larger and more real in both girls' minds. Pam knew that her own rising excitement and sense of anticipation were shared by Penny. Pam had been hoping they wouldn't have to take part-time jobs at school in order to get by financially. She felt the bright luster of college would be dimmed a little by the need to work in free time that might otherwise have been spent in social activity.

But Mother assured them that this wouldn't be necessary. "I can manage quite well," she insisted. "It'll be hard enough for you to keep up your studies the first year. And I want you both to have fun in the spare time you do have. Besides, Howard House is doing just fine. In fact," she admitted with a little smile, "I've even decided to expand a bit."

"How expand?" Pam asked. And Penny, too, waited interestedly for Mother's answer.

"Ty Shelton," Mother explained, "has just about persuaded me to handle the Shelton line of custom-made furniture through Howard House. He doesn't want to enlarge his own plant and an outlet and show space are what he needs most. So it might work out very well for both of us."

Pam leaned over to confide in a clearly audible whisper to Penny, "*That's* why he hangs around so much and has to take her out to dinner so often."

And Penny nodded with mock gravity and whispered back, "Strictly business, of course!"

"All right, you two," Mother laughed.

"And to think," Pam said, "it all began with a pair of loveseats!"

Which was quite true. The first time Celia had met Ty Shelton, she had driven out to the furniture company he owned, which was located in a small town on the Fox River, not too far from Glenhurst. Shelton's had a fine name for very good reproductions of period pieces, the sort which Celia often needed for decorating jobs. But her first encounter with Mr. Tyrone Shelton had been a stormy one. She came home that evening quite annoyed, but full of fabulous details about the Shelton Company and its unusual proprietor. Pam and Penny heard all about her experiences over dinner. It seemed the factory was very old, having been founded almost a hundred years before.

"And I don't think it's been changed much since," Mother announced. "There's even an old mill-wheel sort of thing out back that they used for power before regular electricity was installed. Quite picturesque. It gives the whole place a kind of old-world charm. But really," Mother went on, a little smile lifting one corner of her mouth, "this man Shelton is a character! He's quite New England-ish. His ancestors came from Vermont, he told me, and he's very laconic and droll—but stubborn!"

Mother had known exactly what she wanted that day she first met Ty Shelton. A pair of Victorian loveseats in a particular shade of rose brocade. But she and Ty had got into a hot argument over proportion and back detail. And not until Mother had been ready to snatch up her sketches and samples and depart had a compromise been worked out. True, she had admitted later, Mr. Shelton's arguments had been sound. He really knew his business. But that, she had supposed, would be the end of their association. Mr. Shelton, it developed, had other ideas.

A few days later he had dropped in at Howard House. He was quite interested in the shop and much more agreeable than he had seemed at first contact. He was impressed with the job Celia had done in remodeling a run-down old house into a smart interior decorating set-up. And the upshot of it all had been Ty Shelton's invitation to Mother and the twins to have dinner with him.

"I was so flabbergasted," Mother admitted afterward to Pam and Penny, "I couldn't think of a way to get out of it gracefully. And he was so nice and sort of sincere, I didn't like to hurt his feelings. He wants to take us all out to some restaurant that used to be a farm, near Dundee. Next Sunday, he suggested. Will you mind awfully?"

"It sounds like fun to me," Pam said.

And Penny nodded, "Sure, why not?"

"Of course," Pam had added with a little teasing laugh, "we know we're only being included as chaperones."

The Sunday afternoon excursion proved to be a very pleasant one. The restaurant to which Ty Shelton drove them in his sleek gray sedan had a great deal of country charm and atmosphere in addition to serving perfectly fabulous food. But Ty Shelton himself was the real reason they all had so much fun. He was, as Celia had told them, both droll and laconic. His thin, rather bony face under a graying shock of sandy hair, lit most attractively with his oddly boyish smile. He had an amusing fund of stories to tell of colorful New Englanders who had been his ancestors, ship captains and workers in wood. One of the latter had been his grandfather, Ezra Shelton, who came West when Chicago was only a village on the edge of a swamp, and was the founder of the Shelton Company.

"In fact," Ty admitted, "Grandfather originally planned to start in business in Chicago. He was offered a chance to buy some property there, but he often told how it was low and soggy and grew nothing but swamp grass as high as a man on a horse, so he refused it. That particular plot of land is where the City Hall stands now," Ty chuckled. "But old Ezra never regretted that he went another fifty miles or so farther west and settled on the Fox River."

"He must have been a rugged individualist like you,"

Celia said drily. "But just think, if he'd decided differently, you might have been a millionaire."

Ty said, "Maybe. Maybe not." There was an amused twinkle in his hazel eyes. "Anyway, millionaires are no longer the happy, carefree souls they used to be, so I guess it's just as well. Besides, I like the furniture business and I'd probably have ended up in real estate if Ezra had started speculating."

Pam and Penny thought Ty Shelton a most interesting person and lots of fun. They told Mother as much later. And she had to agree he was likeable when you got to know him and that the afternoon had been a pleasant one. Ty was a frequent visitor at Howard House after that. And now, only a few weeks later, Celia was telling the twins that she had decided to sell some of the Shelton line of furniture through Howard House.

"Would you be partners?" Penny asked interestedly.

"Oh, no," Mother shook her head. "Howard House is all ours. Ty wouldn't have a thing to do with it. He just doesn't want to expand, or have his company grow any bigger. It suits him fine as it is. Still, he's cramped for showroom space, so Howard House seems a logical outlet for a part of his line."

Pam nodded. She said then, her tone teasing, "We just wanted to be sure it was strictly a business deal. He hangs around so much, we were beginning to wonder."

And Penny added, in a mock regretful voice, "Ty isn't nearly as spectacular as Paul Gerard, though. And Mother didn't fall for him, fascinating as he was. So I guess there's not much chance Ty will take her off our hands, either."

"You're stuck with me," Celia smiled. "Might as well face the fact."

"Remember how we got our hopes up when Paul was giving her such a rush?" Pam went on with the teasing.

But it hadn't, she recalled, actually been that way at all. She had been downright worried over Mother's interest in Randy's attractive uncle, who was a well-known newspaper correspondent and had been visiting the Kirkpatricks while he worked on a book. But Mother's friendship with Paul had come to nothing, no hearts had been broken when he went abroad once more. Still, Pam remembered vividly the qualms of uneasiness she herself had suffered over the situation. Penny had been more philosophical about it. And Pam, too, had wanted Mother to be happy. But she had hated the idea of any drastic change in their agreeable way of life. And she had been secretly relieved at Paul's departure and the fact that Mother's only contact with him now was an infrequent card from some exotic foreign place.

Although Ty Shelton was around even more often after his and Celia's business connection became an accomplished fact, the twins weren't too concerned. Mother's friendship with Paul Gerard had been much more exciting. Paul used to take Celia to the theater, or dancing, to send her red roses. Ty was more likely to call up and invite himself to dinner, offering to bring along the main items of food. He would stop at a farm en route and arrive laden with a plump spring chicken, red-ripe tomatoes and delicious berries, country butter and eggs. He loved to cook and would insist on taking over the job of frying the chicken, while Celia and the girls attended to the vegetables and the salad and sundry other—in Ty's opinion—less important details. Then they would eat most informally around the table in the dining nook. Sometimes there would be the four of them, often their number might be augmented by Mike or Randy or both. Occasionally there were just Celia and Ty. Gran and Lucius also developed a warm liking for Mother's new friend and business associate and many were the hotly contested bridge games that ensued between them.

Before long, it was hard for Pam and Penny to remember how it had been before Ty Shelton loomed on their horizon. Scarcely a week passed that they didn't see him once or twice. But his infiltration into their lives and Mother's was so gradual and easy they hardly noticed it. He was just Ty, coming and going, sometimes on a business errand, sometimes just stopping in for no special reason.

The twins' minds were too full of college plans to absorb much of anything else. They had already begun to assemble their clothes, and in this project Gran proved most helpful. She was a wonderful seamstress and loved to sew, which meant that Pam's and Penny's clothes expenditures could be held to a minimum. Each of them already had a fine collection of hand-knit sweaters, thanks to Gran. And the skirts and suits she tailored for them, the dresses she fashioned so artfully, were the equal of those of any of their friends, purchased ready-made for a good deal more money.

"We're lucky having Gran," Penny said once. "We can get twice as many nice things as we could afford otherwise."

And Pam agreed, "Don't see how we'd manage without her."

They spent a good deal of time at Gran's and Lucius'

big, comfortable old house, for fittings and conferences as to style and material. Gran was as enthusiastic about it all as the twins. And Lucius, too, seemed to get a kick out of their company. Afterwards, the girls talked about that marriage.

"They're so cute together, aren't they?" Pam said.

And Penny agreed, "You can tell they're happy. And they seem younger, somehow. Not that either of them ever was exactly decrepit, but now they're both even gayer and more full of pep. And they get such a bang out of doing things together, even if it's only gardening or something perfectly ordinary."

Pam said, "Lucius is like a new person. Remember the kind of wistful way he used to hang around here, as if he were warming his hands against being lonely? And he was so grateful to us for including him in things."

"Now he and Gran have a life of their own," Penny said.

"That's for sure," Pam chuckled. "Did you hear them talking about maybe going on a cruise this fall?"

Penny nodded, smiling. "I'm glad things worked out so that they have each other."

Pam found herself wondering, as she had occasionally wondered before, whether Mother, too, would be happier if she re-married. Of course, Mother was busy and content. She had them and her work to keep her occupied. She had a lot of friends and was asked out frequently to parties and for bridge. And yet—

"You know what I sometimes wonder, Pam?" Penny's thoughtful voice broke into Pam's reflections.

Pam nodded. "Whether Mother ever gets lonely, too."

It wasn't unusual for their thoughts to travel a similar course and arrive simultaneously at the same destination. But they sat silent now, for neither of them knew the answer to the question that had come into both their minds.

10 *Straight Talk*

ONE point about Harwood still rankled in Pam's mind, the fact that there were no sororities or fraternities there. She had known this when she agreed to go, but whenever she thought of it, disappointment welled up anew.

"I've always dreamed of joining a sorority," she mourned. "Rush Week and being pledged—it all sounds so heavenly."

"But there are lots of clubs at Harwood," Penny reminded her anxiously. "And everyone gets to join the one they're most interested in. It's really more democratic that way. And ever so many colleges don't permit secret societies any more."

"Ever so many still do," Pam griped. "But I have to let myself be talked into going to one of the other kind."

Penny's gray eyes were troubled. "I suppose," she said, "if you don't like it there, you can transfer to another school next year—or we can—" her hesitation indicated she was feeling the cross-pull of two loyalties, one toward Pam and one toward Mike.

Pam's resentment over Mike's influence on Penny had dulled somewhat, at least enough for her to feel a twinge of sympathy for her twin. Still, she felt a bit sorry for herself, too. She said grumpily, "I'll try it this year. But I'm not making any rash promises to stay on if I don't like it."

"Of course not," Penny said. "I wouldn't expect you to. But I think we're all going to like it there, you and Mike and I. I've got a sort of hunch about it."

"Optimist," Pam said drily . . .

In a way the days seemed to fly and in another to drag. Pam was eager to start college, yet she clung to the familiarity of home, of known friends, of customary activities. The mid-summer weather was very warm and Pam went as often as she could to the country club with Randy and the crowd. They played a little tennis, swam in the azure-lined pool and sunned themselves to a ripe golden tan. Or they might simply relax in comfortable chairs on the shaded terrace, drinking tall tinkling concoctions and talking lazily on any number of subjects. But eventually the talk always seemed to drift to college.

"Isn't it a fascinating prospect?" Laurie McGregor exclaimed one August afternoon. "It'll be so different!"

"Studying, you mean?" Mitch Martin cracked.

"That's not the part I'm looking forward to," Laurie laughed. "Although if I don't keep up my grades, my father will skin me. But when I think of getting up to New York on week-ends to see the new plays and dance at all the famous places—" she broke off, turning her warm blue glance on Randy, who was sitting between her and Pam. "Will you look me up when you're at Cornell?

It's quite close, you know, and we can keep each other from getting homesick."

"Why, sure," Randy said casually. "I'll do that."

"You won't mind, Pam?" Laurie's tone was honeyed. "He can't spend all his time just studying and writing to you."

"You have my blessing," Pam smiled. "Randy may not be planning to write to me at all."

"Oh, I figured on wasting a spare minute now and then," Randy said lightly, "just to keep in touch."

But his eyes said something much deeper, Pam realized, even as she kidded back, "And if I have a spare minute, I'll answer."

She wondered, though, as she spoke the casual words, whether they were true. Maybe it would be better to break up entirely when they separated to go to college. She hadn't looked ahead beyond this summer, other than to imagine a sort of easy, undemanding friendship continuing between them. But maybe such a relationship wasn't possible from Randy's angle. Was it unfair to him, Pam wondered, to simply let things drift, as she was satisfied to do? Or did she owe it to Randy to be honest, as Penny had insisted?

The question was to rise in her mind many times as the summer slipped away. But Pam avoided trying to find an answer to it. Let things ride, she told herself, so long as Randy didn't demand a showdown. Have fun right now, this minute, and let the future take care of itself.

But on a brooding late-summer night, with storm clouds blacking out the moon like a dropped curtain and thin, too bright veins of lightning forking across the sky,

Pam found herself confronted with the necessity of making a decision and letting Randy know exactly how things stood.

There had been one of the regular monthly dances at the country club that Saturday night and Pam had gone to it with Randy. This had been their first date in more than a week, since Pam had been letting Joe Henderson monopolize a bit more than his share of her time. With Joe, there was no problem. Their dates were simply for kicks, from his angle as well as hers. Randy had seemed a bit hurt and sulky all evening.

A lot of the crowd were there and the dance had been fun, despite Randy's quietness. The music and soft lights, the summery pastel colors of the girls' clothes, interspersed with the sharp black and white of male attire, wove a kind of pattern for Pam, familiar, but never tiresome. And yet, under the thin layer of her pleasure, there was an uneasy awareness of Randy's dark gaze, brooding on her, of the insistently possessive touch of his hand on her arm, or close about her waist as they danced. By the time they were ready to start home the night had turned windy and an occasional rumble of thunder sounded ominously.

"It's going to storm," Randy said, moving to raise his convertible's top.

But Pam demurred, "Leave it down till it starts."

Randy grinned, sliding in beside her. "Want to live dangerously? You may get drenched if it comes in a hurry."

Pam said, "My dress is cotton. It can take it."

As the car swung out of the curving country club drive

onto the road, Randy informed her, "We're going for a ride."

Pam had been cagey about letting herself in for long, solitary conversations with Randy. But tonight she didn't object. Something in his manner made it plain he wouldn't have listened.

He told her now, "We've been making like a pair of ostriches lately, burying our heads in the sand."

Pam couldn't deny it. "I guess we have, Randy."

He drove on, not very fast, at a steady pace that made conversation safe and easy. Lightning cut a greenish streak down the black sky and a moment later thunder rumbled. The trees along the road whipped and groaned in the wind and Pam snuggled deeper into the warmth of her light fleece jacket. But she liked the wind in her hair, the elements threatening. They were somehow akin to her mood.

Randy said, his voice low but firm, "I think it's time we had a straight talk, Pam. We've got to settle things between us."

Pam nodded. Maybe it would be better that way. Maybe then she could get rid of the sense of guilt she felt when she thought about Randy. She explained, "I hoped we could just drift through this summer and then things would settle themselves."

"I know," Randy said. "You were fairly obvious about it. Never see me alone for more than a few unavoidable minutes, not give me too much of your time, keep our conversations on a completely trivial level—that was your system, wasn't it?"

Pam felt warm color wash across her face. Randy was

more perceptive than she had realized. But if he had been aware of her tactics, why had he appeared to let her get away with them?

As if sensing the question in her mind, he went on, "I told you I'd been playing ostrich, too. Even though I saw through you, I've been afraid of a showdown. If I dragged everything out into the open, it might mean I wouldn't be seeing you any more—" His husky voice stopped and the night was still, except for the rush of wind about the car, the more insistent thunder.

Then Pam said slowly and with complete honesty, "Randy, I like you so very much, I don't want to hurt you. I'm perfectly willing to go on being friends—but if our friendship has to be spoiled by you wanting it more serious and my trying to put you off all the time—well, it's no good, is it?"

"Not for me," Randy said. "I can't take it."

"It's no good for me, either," Pam's voice was gentle, grave. "Because then I begin to hate myself for—deceiving you, stringing you along. Friends shouldn't do that to each other, so I don't want to do it to you. It's different with the other boys. They're no more serious than I am." She asked then, a faint note of regret in her tone, "Oh, Randy, why couldn't we have been like that, too?"

"Kept it gay, you mean?" His mouth twisted a little. Pam saw the bitter set of it in a sudden flash of lightning. "Because I had to go and fall in love with you. Don't ask me why. I know eighteen's too young to fall in love, as well as you do. The only thing is, if you could give me some hope for later—" the pleading note in his voice touched her heart.

"Randy," Pam cried, "I'm sorry. But you want me to

be honest, don't you? I'm ashamed of the way I've acted. I like you better than any other boy I know—but I'm not in love with you. I don't think I ever will be."

Randy argued, "Eighteen's too young for you to be sure. Just think about it once in awhile. Wait till Christmas vacation—"

But Pam broke in, insisting, "Randy, I am sure! Waiting won't change anything. You mustn't keep on hoping."

Neither of them had been paying much attention to the impending storm. Now, abruptly the heavens seemed to open and dump their burden of very wet contents over the world with complete abandon. Randy stopped the car and got the top raised in a minute, but not before Pam's hair was plastered around her face and his own white dinner jacket clung wetly to his shoulders.

"You see," Pam said with a rather shaky laugh, "I tell the truth and it brings on a cloudburst."

"Better watch that," Randy told her.

As he swung the car around and headed toward home, Pam said seriously, "If you're going to figure I'll change my mind, I'm not going out with you any more, Randy."

Not until then did Randy tell her, "This is our last date for a long time, anyway. I'm leaving tomorrow."

"For college?" Pam asked in surprise. "But it's too soon."

"Mother and Dad are going to drive with me," he explained. "We'll take our time, make a tour of it, stop in New York and Washington. And I'll end up at Cornell. They've been wanting to do that and just lately I've decided it might be a good thing."

"It's—quite a surprise," Pam admitted.

Weeks of the summer left and no Randy. She felt a sudden sense of loss—or was it just shock at the unexpectedness of his going? Pam wasn't sure. Her feelings were confused, mixed up.

"So you see," Randy said, "it'll be Christmas before we get together again. And a lot of things can happen by Christmas."

They were rather quiet, driving the rest of the way home.

"Kiss me good-bye?" Randy asked, as they lingered in the cool darkness of Howard House's little entrance porch.

"Oh, Randy," Pam said and went into his arms.

As their lips met, Pam thought, This is the last time.

And her throat felt queer and chokey and her eyelids stung. And, perversely, Randy's kiss was more unsettling than it had been in a long, long time . . .

Everyone wanted to have a final party during those last, too short days of the waning summer. The tempo of the twins' social life increased to a dizzy pace. And yet there were moments in between when Pam found herself thinking of Randy, missing him more than she had expected to. But she never admitted it aloud.

At every festivity, college was the main topic of conversation. But underneath all the gay anticipatory chatter a kind of nostalgic regret for the lost familiar pattern of high school days lingered unvoiced and unacknowledged. No one would have dreamed of admitting that he felt faint qualms of uneasiness over the drastic changes ahead. But all of them knew that life suddenly seemed quite wonderful, this moment, this second. And there was an instinct to cling to the present, to wish each day had more hours, each hour more minutes, even while they pretended that they could scarcely wait for the moment of their departure for college.

Celia Howard sensed this. And one evening, talking with Ty Shelton as they lingered over coffee after Pam and Penny had gone off on their respective dates, she tried to put some small part of this feeling, this realization, into words.

She said, smiling a little, "They're just a shade apprehensive about the changes college will bring, even while they're rushing pell-mell to meet them."

"That's a very human attitude," Ty pointed out.

"I suppose so," Celia said. "And yet this is one of the times when being a mother isn't much fun. You wish you could fend off the changes and keep things just as they have been, even while you realize that nothing is static, that new experiences like leaving home for college are a part of the pattern of growing up, of becoming an adult emotionally, as well as merely in the physical sense."

Thoughtfully Ty contemplated the glowing end of his cigarette. "I don't think you have to worry about Pam and Penny. They'll do all right."

"I think so too," Celia smiled across the table at him, "but, of course, I could be prejudiced."

"Not me," Ty denied. "I'm just a crusty old bachelor looking on from the sidelines. But I never could get too worried about the younger generation. Sometimes I wonder if our contemporaries don't expect a bit too much of the kids. They haven't got an easy row to hoe, if you ask me. The boys with army service ahead, trying to fit their education in piecemeal, never being sure whether they'll make it, or if they'll be yanked out of school and put into uniform. And the girls are bound to be affected, too, by this uneasiness, this uncertainty. They don't know what they can count on any more. And unless they've got the right sense of values—well, they could go haywire for fair."

"A sense of values," Celia repeated. "That's what I hope I've helped Pam and Penny acquire. In the long run, I guess that's the most important thing parents can hand on to their children." She went on, a faint smile touching her lips, "It's funny in a way. It used to be Penny I worried most about. She was so unsure of herself. But Penny's all right now. Maybe she was always all right in important ways. She has a kind of inner strength that I sometimes wonder if Pam lacks."

Ty told Celia, "I don't think you need to worry about Pam, either. She's more mature than Penny in some ways, but younger in others. She's growing up all the time, though. Maybe you're too close to see it, but I can."

"I hope you're right," Celia said. "She still seems so dazzled with fun and dates and lots of beaux, all the surface glitter. Do you suppose she'll get over that at college?"

"Give her time," Ty chuckled. "Who was the sage who once said that there was nothing wrong with youth that growing older wouldn't cure?"

As she laughed with him, Celia felt a warm little glow of gratitude for Ty's friendship, his sound common sense. Without him, she faced the fact that she would have dreaded the twins' imminent departure for college even more than she did.

11 *College Is Different*

THOSE first days at college were at once an uprooting and a transplanting and it was hard to tell just when one stage stopped and the other began. There was the initial rush and jumble of enrollment in classes and assignment to rooms, of placement tests, of trying to get settled and learning to find one's way around. Everything seemed strange and just a little forbidding. New classrooms. New teachers. New methods and procedures. And underneath it all the sharp pangs of homesickness, the longing for familiar faces, the sick surety deep down inside that you would never get used to all this.

Pam and Penny and Mike were grateful for each other to take the keen edge off all this newness, this strangeness. At first the three of them seemed like a small island battered by alien seas. But gradually and almost without their realizing what was happening, their horizons broadened, so that they no longer felt alone and lost when they were apart from each other. All of them made new acquaintances who quickly became friends. They found the campus and even the small town of Harwood growing as familiar as the streets of Glenhurst. And the nostalgia for their old surroundings faded imperceptibly until it was quite gone.

Home became for Pam a second-floor bedroom in Grace Kirkland Hall, one of the freshman girls' dormitories. A small room whose impersonal furnishings of bed and dresser and desk and chair were made warmer and more cheerful by Pam's choice of yellow spread and curtains, of white shag rugs and gay pictures. Penny's room was just beyond, with a connecting door. All the bedrooms at Grace Kirkland were arranged in two-room suites and the twins were delighted to be able to share such close living quarters.

As they had in high school, each made her own special friends, among girls whose tastes and interests most closely matched her own. But the fact that these outside associations were with quite different types of girls in no way affected Pam's and Penny's closeness to each other.

Pam's best friend was Marylou Ritter, a slender, angelic-looking blonde who lived across the hall. Marylou's fragile appearance was deceptive and completely at variance with her boundless energy and enthusiasm. Penny's particular crony was Ellen Carr, whom she met in English I and who shared her own avid interest in books and writing. Penny found Marylou quite flamboyant and shallow and Pam considered quiet, brown-haired Ellen dull. But both twins adopted a live-and-let-live attitude and refrained from derogatory comment.

"Maybe," Pam said once with a little laugh, "that's a sign of maturity. Do you suppose? Remember how I used to try to talk you into going with my crowd at high school? And they bored you stiff, but I still couldn't see why you preferred the friends you picked for yourself. And I couldn't keep my mouth shut about it, either."

Penny smiled, too, remembering. "I suppose it's always hard for twins to realize they're not as much alike on the inside as they are out."

"Since we do, we get along better," Pam said. And added then, quite frankly, "I sort of resented it when you began thinking things out for yourself instead of just following my ideas. It's kind of flattering to have someone depend on you and I missed it when you stopped. I even blamed Mike for awhile—I guess I figured in some crazy way that he'd come between us."

"Oh, Pam!" Penny exclaimed. "You don't any longer?"

Pam shook her head. "Now I know better. I've developed quite a sisterly attitude toward Mike. I like him as well as ever—but differently."

"I'm glad," Penny said. And her tone was light. Still, Pam sensed that she really meant it . . .

The Harwood College buildings were an assortment of types, depending upon the period in which they had been constructed. There was Old Hall, one of the first buildings to be erected after Harwood had been chartered by the Ohio state legislature back in 1850. Turreted and dingy, it thrust up from its shawl of trees like a wizened old woman draped in a too gay and youthful bit of finery. And like a jeweled hat-ornament, the bell in the tower, which had called the very first classes together, caught the sun's gleam and reflected it dazzlingly in the late afternoon.

In sharpest contrast to Old Hall there was the Music

Building, finished less than a year ago, cleanly modern and functional in design. And in between the two the rest of the college buildings tried to adapt themselves to both without too much conflict. Pam supposed that most colleges were like that, really. Something of a hodge-podge architecturally. But at least there was a feeling of space and serenity about the Harwood campus. There were sweeps of lawn and winding paths and even some ivy in the true classic tradition.

Pam preferred the newer buildings. She was glad Old Hall was used only to house the school's historical treasures and early records. The place was a veritable museum of antiquity, with a musty, distinctive smell, a landmark without which most Harwood students were agreed the old school wouldn't seem the same.

But Pam had exclaimed at her first glimpse of it, "What a relic! It looks haunted."

Penny had answered, smiling, "Only by the nicest, most gentle ghosts then. I think it just looks sort of sleepy and dreaming, as if it's living in the past."

"I'll take the present," Pam had said drily.

She found, somewhat to her own surprise, that she liked the shape and form of her new life and that Harwood was proving more satisfactory than she had been willing to let herself expect. Of course, there was a lot of studying to do, but that was probably the case at any college. And Pam didn't seem to mind studying so much any more. Her subjects were proving more interesting than they had in high school. The teachers were, for the most part, stimulating, and their give-and-take attitude toward the students made classes lively as well as informative. Not that Pam would ever be an outstanding student. Still, she felt she was doing quite well. Penny scarcely had to help her at all.

A new and more mature sense of responsibility grew in her. Knowing the effort Mother was making to see them both through college, Pam found herself sharing Penny's urge to take as full advantage of their opportunities as possible. Not, of course, that they didn't mean to have fun, too. Especially Pam.

Penny and Mike joined the Journalism Club, Pam the Drama Club. She found some of her fellow members much more congenial than others. Along with Marylou, Pam became an integral part of a small, exclusive clique of girls, one in which she felt lucky to be included. Most of the others had more money than she, their clothes bore the labels of expensive shops in Louisville and Dallas and Detroit and Chicago. Yet Pam was at ease with them, she fitted in, just as she had gravitated naturally to the top crowd back at Glen High.

"They're probably the most popular crowd," Mike said one afternoon when he and Penny and Pam were walking together across campus toward the dormitory. "But they're certainly not the most intelligent. Or aren't brains fashionable this season?"

"Oh, I don't know," Pam said. "It takes brains to get by with as little studying as some of them do and not be flunked out."

"All I hope," Mike told her, "is that their attitude isn't catching. You're so young and susceptible."

Pam made a face at him and Penny remarked, "She's been doing fine, Mike. Don't pick on her."

"Shhh!" Mike pretended to look around fearfully. "Some of her pals might hear you. And if they know she's keeping up her grades, they'll probably have nothing more to do with her."

"All right," Pam told him drily, "you can stop making like a big brother with all the subtly camouflaged advice. I'll get by. Don't worry . . ."

As usual, Pam had plenty of dates. She and the other girls in her crowd attracted the most popular and sought-after male students. In view of which, it was a rather curious circumstance that Pam should have met Cade Venner through Penny. Penny's part in the affair was indirect, still there was no denying it.

One day in late September Pam came out of her English Lit class onto the sun-drenched campus where drifts of brown leaves skittered drily underfoot. There was a faint tang of wood-smoke on the air and the sky was a clear bright blue. Pam felt a detaining hand on her elbow and a deep voice asked, "What's your rush?"

Pam turned in surprise to look up into a rather narrow dark face with a shock of close-cut black hair bristling above it. Bold brown eyes beneath strongly marked brows stared down into hers as the young man added, "Well, don't act so startled. I borrowed your text-book in Chemistry this morning. Doesn't that constitute an introduction, or are we going to be stuffy about it?"

Pam smiled then, denying, "Sorry, but I don't take Chemistry." Penny did, though, so she sensed the mistake he was making. And far be it from her to lose out on such a made-to-order opportunity to get acquainted with the most attractive man she had so far encountered at Harwood and one who had long intrigued her attention.

The dark young man's brows drew closer together and

he glowered at her. "What is this, a brush-off? I sat next to you for an hour. I guess I ought to know."

Pam went on smiling in the face of his obvious disgruntlement. She said, "Could be it was my sister you sat next to. My twin sister."

"You kidding me?"

Pam shook her head. "If you check, you'll find her name's Penny Howard. I'm Pam."

"I'm Cade Venner," the young man supplied.

"I know," Pam admitted. "I've heard your name mentioned in English Lit."

"Heard me getting the pants bawled off me," Cade Venner said unconcernedly. He grinned then and Pam thought how different his face was in amusement, more open, younger looking, less tense. He said, "How about that? I never knew any twins before. You two sure look alike. A regular double feature."

"So we've been told," Pam agreed. "Although double feature is a new way of putting it. We've been called carbon copies, though, and a case of seeing double and stuff like that."

"How's a guy supposed to tell you apart?" Cade asked.

"It isn't so hard," Pam said, "when you get to know us. There are little differences."

"Maybe when I see you together," Cade nodded. "Have to arrange that. It'd be interesting." He added then, quite casually, "How about a Coke at the Union?"

"Both of us?" Pam asked. "Or just me? I'm afraid Penny's clear across campus at the library right now."

Cade Venner chuckled as they started to walk on together. "You'll do for this time. I'll take on the two of you later . . ."

12   *Cade Venner*

P_AM_ stood at her bedroom window, watching chill October rain sluice down over the campus. The sodden lawn and meandering white-graveled path looked singularly deserted and uninviting. At the top of the Music Building steps, a group of students huddled, waiting for the downpour to lessen. Above everything the clouds drooped in a gray velvet canopy, low and threatening. Water blurred the glass before Pam, making the clump of waiting students appear to run together like paints on a damp palette.

"Darn!" she exclaimed aloud in sharp annoyance, although there was no one around to hear. "Oh, darn!"

She had wanted to escape this afternoon before Penny got back from her final class of the day. Penny knew about the long Spanish translation that Pam had shrugged aside sleepily last night, murmuring, "I'll have time for it tomorrow afternoon." And while Penny might not say it in so many words, she'd feel Pam should have remembered it and taken it into her calculations instead of agree-

ing to meet Cade Venner at four o'clock at the Student
Union.

The situation was complicated by the fact that Pam,
with customary carelessness, had left her raincoat at the
library. She had meant to stop by for it on her way back
to her room to freshen up before her meeting with Cade.
But it hadn't been raining just then and Pam had been in
a towering hurry. And now this sudden drenching downpour had her trapped and Penny would be coming in any
minute and there would be explanations and further de-
lay. And Cade wasn't, Pam knew with an excited little
flutter in her throat, the type you kept waiting very long.

Footsteps sounded in the hall and Pam turned from the
window, thinking it must be Penny. But through the
open doorway she saw with relief that it was Marylou
Ritter.

"Hi, honeychile," Marylou called, glimpsing Pam at
the same moment. She stood there, her raincoat dripping
water onto the hall floor as she added superfluously, "It's
wet outside."

"Angel!" Pam exclaimed, her eyes lighting.

"Not I," Marylou denied. "Got no wings, got no halo."

"Got a raincoat, though." Pam moved toward her pur-
posefully. "And that's more use to me right now. I'm
supposed to be meeting Cade at the Union this minute.
And here I am, stuck, and Penny's out and wearing her
raincoat."

"Inconsiderate of her, isn't it?" Marylou chuckled.
"Here, you're welcome to it." She slipped out of the pale
green plastic coat and Pam took it and put it on, murmuring hasty thanks. "Don't say I ever stood in the way of a

girl meeting Cade Venner. If you can't make 'em bat an eyelash yourself, help your friends snare 'em, that's my motto. Bless you, my child. Don't shoot till you can see the whites of his eyes and remember to keep your ammunition dry—with my raincoat." The light gay voice followed after Pam as she ran down the hall.

She took the stairs in a quick swoop, hurried across the big entrance hall and went out into the chill rain. As she hurried along, she pulled the raincoat's loose hood up around her head so that it sealed her into a little quiet world of detached withdrawal. Her feet were light on the graveled path, the cement sidewalk, skirting the puddles automatically. Her thoughts were all of Cade. Would he still be waiting, she wondered?

Never before had Pam felt so deliciously unsure of a man, so uncertain as to how he might react to any situation. But then, never had she known a man like Cade. He was older, for one thing, than the boys Pam had previously dated. Although a freshman, he had behind him a period of active service with the Marines, in which he had enlisted straight out of high school. He had served in Japan and Korea, coming through it all without a scratch, affected only in inner ways not visible to the naked eye.

Cade was unpredictable, sometimes in Pam's opinion unfathomable. Always before she had been able, after a few dates, to sense exactly what made a man tick, to know the combination that unlocked his personality. But not Cade Venner. Just when you thought you had him figured out, he did something that upset all the conclusions you had arrived at so laboriously and you realized that you didn't actually know him at all.

That, Pam supposed, sloshing along toward the Student Union, was in part what made him so fascinating. Practically every girl she knew would have jumped at the chance of a date with Cade. The fact that he could pick and choose made it all the more flattering when he singled you out for attention. And single her out was exactly what he had done, Pam thought with a little smile, from that day weeks ago when they'd met.

But even now, after a dozen dates and numerous casual encounters in class or at the Union, there were still moments when she realized with a small exciting sense of shock that Cade was still a stranger. There were inner depths in him, fastnesses not to be penetrated or explored in a few weeks' time. He was an anomaly, inconsistent, unreasonable at times, given to quick almost frightening rages, but gay and sweet when the spirit moved him. And always fascinating—

Pam's thoughts were interrupted by the sudden beep of a car horn close beside her, a slow, drawling sort of voice calling out, "Want a lift, lady?"

She looked up and it was Jeff Moore, driving his disreputable-looking old panel truck. He had stopped at the curb beside her and was holding the door open invitingly. Jeff was a friend of Mike Bradley's and Pam had double-dated with him and Penny and Mike a couple of times. He was nice enough, but not exciting like Cade. Jeff, too, was a veteran who had come to college a bit older than the average run of freshmen. He didn't live on campus at all, but drove back and forth every day from the farm some twenty-five miles away, where he lived with his family. Jeff was a big young man, with a solid jaw and a way of looking out of half-closed hazel eyes, as though he found life vastly interesting in a quiet way, but wanted to appraise things before taking them too seriously. He had medium brown hair and a deep tan that almost matched it.

Pam liked him well enough, but now she found the sight of him and his messy old truck almost equally distasteful. Her mind had been so full of Cade, her every instinct had been propelling her so forcefully toward their meeting, that Jeff's amiable grin, his offer of a ride, seemed like nothing but untimely interruptions. Particularly with her destination looming a scant half a block ahead.

She called out, forcing an answering smile, "Oh, thanks, Jeff, but I'm only heading for the Union."

Jeff said, "Too bad I didn't catch up with you sooner." He lifted a big hand in cheerful farewell, shifted gears and went on, the old truck lumbering noisily down the street.

Pam thought disdainfully, I'd rather walk in the rain than ride in that wreck. It probably smells of pigs.

She had gained the entry of the Union Building by that time. As she went in, a wave of talk and laughter, of juke box music and the friendly clink of soft drink bottles, broke over her. Pam slipped out of Marylou's raincoat and moved forward eagerly, her glance sweeping the enormous crowded lounge in expectant darts. People spoke to her and she answered, yet there was a curious feeling of unfulfillment in her, a sense of desperate seeking. It was as if, until she found Cade in all this press of unimportant people, none of them had the power to penetrate her abstraction, to make any lasting impression on her.

As though, Pam thought with a queer little half-panicky feeling, I haven't any identity without Cade, as if I'm only half a person until I find him.

There was something disturbing in the thought. Never before had any man been so important to Pam. Always until now, she had been the vital part in any relationship, she had held the reins of any previous association firmly and competently in her own two hands. Now she seemed to have lost that firm control, which always before she had taken so casually for granted.

Cade, Cade, her heart cried out, where are you? Why didn't you wait for me?

He wasn't in their favorite corner booth where they usually met, although Pam's anxious glance returned to it again and again. He wasn't with the noisy, laughing crowd around the big circular counter and soda fountain. She couldn't see him in any of the shifting, chattering groups. He wasn't anywhere. And then Pam's heart lifted swiftly with relief and delight. Across the intervening heads, the meaningless faces, her searching gaze found a tall, slumped figure, a brooding dark face, a cropped black head. Cade was standing at the juke box, morosely feeding a coin into it.

And as Pam flew toward him, she thought surely the rain outside must have ceased and the sun must have broken through the overhanging clouds, because it was as though the whole world brightened with her finding him.

13

At the Student Union

"CADE," Pam said, coming up to him a trifle breathlessly and touching his arm, "I'm sorry I'm late."

He turned to glance at her without surprise, without even a gleam of welcome in his dark glance. "You late?"

Pam said, teasing, "Okay. If you're going to be like that, I won't even apologize."

"Never apologize," Cade told her with polite gravity. "It puts you in the wrong. Lesson Number One in the Technique of Knocking a Guy for a Loop. You should have said, "Cade, darling, you're early!" That would have taken the wind out of my sails before I had a chance to give you what for."

"So now are you going to?" Pam laughed up at him from under her eyelashes.

"Going to what?" Cade asked, still perfectly dead-pan.

"Give me what for," Pam said.

"Save it, baby," Cade suggested. "All that soft-talk and big-eye routine may go over great with these diapered

infants who are your contemporaries. But I'm a big boy,
remember? And when a girl says she'll meet me at four
o'clock, I expect her by four and no amount of very skill-
ful female flirting is going to make me forget I got a gripe.
See?" Cade asked.

Pam found herself explaining humbly, "I really
couldn't help it, though. It was raining so hard and I was
caught without a raincoat. I had to borrow Marylou's to
get here."

"So I'm not worth getting pneumonia for?" Cade
smiled at her at last. "Well, I'll forgive you this time.
But don't let it happen again."

He put his arm behind her, his hand casually on
her shoulder, and propelled her toward the corner booth.
People spoke to them both as they passed, the usual
friendly, stereotyped greetings. "Hi, there." "How's
things?" "What's new?" But in every girl's eye that lifted
to Cade's, Pam saw a quick gleam of interest. And they
looked at her with envy, hidden, of course, in the politely
civilized manner. But it was there just the same. Pam saw
it, sensed it, and was pleased and proud. She doubted that
there was a girl in that big, crowded room, who wouldn't
have been happy to change places with her, to have
Cade's hand resting in that casually proprietary manner
on her shoulder. And Pam thrilled to his touch and
gloried in the envy.

There were several of their friends in the corner booth,
and they moved over willingly to make room for Pam and
Cade. Too great a show of enthusiasm was considered
naive by this crowd. Their attitude of detached boredom
set them distinctively apart from the majority of their
fellow students. Yet they were tolerant of Pam's natural

gayety and vivacity. Having her in the crowd seemed to contribute to the general pleasure. Her knack for enjoying things fully tended to enliven the somewhat jaded tastes of the others.

Cade was easily the most jaded of them all. This, Pam suspected, was largely due to his background. The Venners, she had learned, were quite wealthy and lived in an enormous house in St. Louis. Cade's mother was dead and his father had re-married. His step-mother, whom Cade referred to as Dolores, was considerably younger than his father and had, Cade suspected and admitted quite frankly, married the elder Venner for his money.

"Why else?" Cade inquired, a bitter twist to his mouth, a supercilious slant to his eyebrows. "She's half his age and a very beautiful dish. But she's smart enough to keep him from realizing she's got an adding machine for a heart, so he's satisfied. It's none of my funeral."

There was an echo of some old pain back of Cade's words when he spoke of his father, of the spectacular Dolores. Pam sensed it there, then wondered if she had imagined it, so quickly was it gone, so immediately was his tone light and wry again.

Cade spoke always as though he were making fun of himself, of her, of everyone and everything. As though nothing were worth taking seriously, or getting excited about. As though life were a kind of bitter joke God had played on the human race. Cade found school rules and traditions silly and childish. He wouldn't wear his freshman cap, he didn't bother with any of the clubs, or go out for any form of athletics. He bitterly resented the school regulation that banned cars among students living on campus. Except in cases of necessity, where an exception was made, there was supposed to be no way to get around this rule. But Cade and a few others, more reckless of consequences than the rest, knew of angles whereby the car rule might be circumvented. If you were lucky and didn't get caught. So far Cade hadn't, in spite of the beautiful gray and red convertible he kept at a garage in Cleveland and used frequently after taking the bus in to that city.

Why he had come to a college like Harwood instead of one of the big universities, Pam wasn't quite sure. She caught the impression, although Cade never came right out and admitted it, that his father had brought some pressure to bear on him. Perhaps he had felt that in a smaller, more conservative school, Cade would have to buckle down to things more, not run so free and wild. But Cade resented every restriction on what he considered his personal liberty. And he delighted in finding ways and means to get away with anything he wanted to get away with. In Pam's eyes his recklessness, his unwillingness to be hemmed in or hampered in any way, but added to his devil-may-care attractiveness. But Penny, she knew, was troubled by it and by Pam's association with Cade.

Pam had an idea that Penny's and Mike's promotion of Jeff Moore, their suggestions of double dates for the four of them, were direct results of this uneasiness on Penny's part. The thought of Jeff, big and easy-going, offering her a lift in his old farm truck a few minutes ago, brought a faint indulgent smile to Pam's lips. He meant well, she supposed.

She sat there, sipping the malted Cade had bought for her, feeling his shoulder pressed against hers in a special intimate way. Everyone was yaking away as usual, arguing and laughing and interrupting each other, waving the straws from their drinks for emphasis. Nothing vitally important was discussed. Teachers and subjects and the prospects of the Harwood football team in Saturday's game.

"That bunch of pantywaists?" Cade said derisively. "They'll lose hands down. I've got a loose twenty to back up my opinion."

One of the other fellows took him up on the bet. Pam felt a furtive wish that Cade wouldn't belittle the Harwood team so devastatingly. True, they often got beaten, but they did try. And she always felt a thrill of partisan pleasure, seeing them lope out onto the field in their red jerseys and big white helmets, with the school band playing and the cheer leaders going through their routines. Cade scoffed at such enthusiasm as infantile. So, when she was with him, Pam kept it to herself.

Time slipped past on the tide of talk and laughter. The crowd in the lounge began to thin out and someone in the corner booth glanced at a watch and to everyone's surprise it was almost dinner time.

A general exodus began now among Pam's crowd. Lipstick was freshened on young mouths, combs were run through hair, possessions were gathered up, raincoats slipped on. Outside the Union in the blue, blue dusk, everyone went their various ways.

The rain had stopped and a chill wind at their backs pushed Pam and Cade along toward Grace Kirkland Hall. Cade's hand held Pam's close and warm in the pocket of his jacket. He was in one of his silent moods. Scarcely a word did he say all the way across the campus. Pam lapsed into quiet, too, since trying to get Cade to talk when he didn't feel like it was no use at all. Might as well save one's breath and let him alone, to work his own devious way out of his abstraction. There was no closeness of spirit in their silence and Pam felt a queer little qualm of desolation, of loneliness. It was as though all the lines of communication between them had been blocked off, as though she had completely lost touch with him, despite the grip of their hands in his pocket. She wondered whether, if she spoke to him, he'd even hear.

"Cade?"

After a long moment, he said, "Huh?"

"I just wanted to be sure you were still there," Pam said softly. "We've walked more than a block without a word."

"I'm here." Cade squeezed her fingers. "I was just thinking."

"About what?" Pam asked, then wished she could snatch the words back.

Cade's voice was cold. "Didn't I ever tell you how I hate to be asked what I'm thinking?"

"I'm sorry," Pam murmured. "It was just—something to say."

"Well, don't say it again," Cade told her rudely. "I don't like to have people prying into my thoughts. What I think's my own business. Dames—you're all alike. Always wanting to take more of a guy than he wants to give you!"

"I don't," Pam said furiously, feeling her temper rise to meet the sudden upflaring of his. She tried to pull her hand away but his fingers closed on it crushingly. She felt tears of rage and pain start to her eyes. "Cade, you're hurting me," she gasped.

He pulled her close against him and she could feel the hard muscular strength of his body, the quick beating of his heart. His arms went around her and his mouth came down on hers, hard, demandingly, although she tried to twist her face away. But after a moment she stopped struggling and gave herself over to the blazing thrill of his kiss. When it was over she felt shaken, weak, there in the close circle of his arms.

His cheek pressed against her hair with unaccustomed tenderness. "Sorry, baby," he said, his voice low, almost crooning. "I wouldn't hurt you for the world. It's my vile temper. It gets the best of me sometimes."

"You're telling me?" Pam said.

But she wasn't angry any more. Cade's kiss had dissipated her anger. She said faintly, "Let me go now. Someone will see us."

"Who cares?" Cade asked. "I don't. Do you? Don't tell me they've got a regulation against kissing on campus. I wouldn't put it past them, though."

But he let her go and Pam tucked her arm through his and they walked along through the windswept dimness. Lights were flowering in all the buildings roundabout, yellow against the grayness.

Pam said, "We'd better hurry. I'll be late for dinner and there's definitely a regulation against that."

"Who cares?" Cade asked again. "So I'm late, so I get a demerit. So do you know how I feel about the comparative importance of demerits in a world that's bowling along toward disaster at a merry clip?"

"I know exactly how you feel," Pam told him. "But whether you think demerits are important or not, if I pile up enough of them, I'll get my week-end privileges taken away."

"A fate worse than death," Cade said gravely. He asked then, "How about after dinner? Meet me then?"

Pam wanted to. She felt the urge to agree rise within her. But the memory of her deferred Spanish translation, of several other pressing tasks left undone, held her back.

"Oh, Cade," she exclaimed regretfully, "I just can't! I'd love to but there's this stinking assignment I've been putting off and—"

"Never mind the excuses," Cade cut in coldly. "There are plenty of other girls."

"Don't be like that—" Pam began.

But he stalked off, leaving her standing there at the steps of Grace Kirkland. The tall slouching figure moved away into the deepening dusk without a word of good-bye, without a gesture.

Pam hated him in that moment. Resentment at his high-handed treatment burned in her. Never in her life had anyone treated her as Cade did. And there was no reason—no earthly reason!—Pam thought furiously, why she should put up with it.

But even as she ran up the steps, blinking hard to keep from crying, Pam knew that she would put up with it— from Cade. When he beckoned again, she would go to him. Pride and anger and resentment might build a high wall about her, but it would crumble at Cade's touch. What was at the root of the dark attraction he held for her, against which she was defenseless?

14 *A Talk with Penny*

PENNY came into Pam's bedroom with a letter in her hand. "From Randy," she said, tossing it to her twin.

Pam glanced at the square white envelope for a minute without interest, almost as though she didn't intend to open it. But then she ran her finger under the flap and took out the single sheet of paper, written all the way down to the bottom in Randy's rather small, concise hand. She read it through and it was much like Randy's other letters had been, informative as to his activities, not too interesting. Neither she nor Randy were very good letter writers, she thought, her mouth twisting in a rather wry smile. No doubt he found her infrequent letters as lifeless and dull as she found his.

"How are things with Randy?" Penny asked, as Pam laid the letter down on the window seat beside her.

"Oh, fine," Pam said casually. She resumed her staring out the window.

It was the week-end of Homecoming. Harwood was overrun with returning alumni and there was much doubling up on sleeping arrangements, so as to accommodate the influx of old graduates. Penny had moved in with Pam from her adjoining room, and perhaps it was this closer, more intimate contact between them that made her so sharply aware of Pam's brooding unhappiness.

She asked now sympathetically, "What is it, Pam? What's the matter?"

"Nothing," Pam said, sitting hunched up on the window seat, her knees under her chin and her arms clasped around them. She was wearing gray slacks and a scarlet blouse, but for all the bright color she looked somber and out-of-sorts and her face seemed pale and pinched. Her glance was fixed on the sunny day beyond the window, on the crowds of students and alumni moving along the campus walks. Yet Penny doubted that she really saw all the movement and color.

"Don't hand me that," Penny said. "I can tell. You've hung around the dorm for days. You wouldn't even go to the bonfire last night—and it was such fun!"

Penny had gone to the bonfire with Mike. They had tried to coax Pam into going along, too, but she had pleaded a headache. Practically everyone had gone to the Homecoming bonfire, she knew. Grace Kirkland had been deserted, there had been an echoing sort of hollowness about the empty rooms and halls. Pam knew because she had lain on her bed in the darkness and listened to the silence, willing the telephone to ring.

Cade wouldn't go to the bonfire, she had been quite sure. Bonfires were kid stuff in Cade's estimation. It would be just like Cade, Pam had thought, to call her up sometime during that particular evening, when everyone else was off watching the towering blaze consuming the great pile of paper and cardboard cartons and wooden crates that most of the students had been gathering and stacking up for days. After the bonfire there was always a snake-dance around the campus and through the streets of the indulgent town. But Cade wouldn't go in for snake-dancing, either.

The phone would ring, Pam had told herself, sounding loud and startling in the stillness of the dorm. And she would answer it and it would be Cade. And he would say approvingly, "Not at the bonfire? You must be growing up, baby." And they would talk and then she would go out to meet him and they would walk somewhere, just the two of them. But they would go to the Union afterward, about the time that the bonfire would have burned itself down to a smouldering pile of ashes and the snake dancers would be stopping by in happy exhaustion to quench their overwhelming thirsts. And everyone would see her with Cade, sitting there in the big corner booth. That sudden gleam of admiration would show in the girls' eyes when they looked at Cade and they would try to conceal their envy of her, but Pam would detect it. And she and Cade would discuss their date for the Homecoming Dance and everything would be just as it had been before Cade got so unreasonably angry with her, before he went stalking off into the dusk last Wednesday without a word or gesture of farewell.

Only—Cade hadn't called.

And Pam had lain there in the dark, with the red glow of the distant bonfire flickering on the walls, with the faint sounds of the faraway revelers reaching her ears, try as she would to shut them out with the bunched-up covers. Everyone had got in quite late. Penny had tried to be quiet, thinking Pam was asleep. Penny had undressed considerately in the dark and had slipped into bed with Pam. There had been a slight scent of wood-smoke in her hair and something warm and comforting about her nearness. But Pam had pretended to be asleep. She hadn't wanted to talk.

She didn't want to talk now. Or she thought she didn't. But suddenly her resistance melted in the face of Penny's whole-hearted sympathy and interest. When you were a twin, it was almost like talking aloud to yourself to tell things to your sister. Pam and Penny had confided in each other for too many years to break the habit now. Pam found herself pouring out all the pent-up resentment she felt against Cade, along with her own confusion as to her reactions to his conduct.

She told Penny, "It's as if I'm an altogether different person where Cade's concerned. You know how I've always been, Pen. I called the shots with Randy and Joe and the rest of the boys I've known. I teased them, flirted with them, tormented them, made them do as I wanted. I came first and it was my wishes that counted. It was selfish of me, but that's how it was. I figured that was the way it always would be. But now, with Cade—" she shrugged and was silent, staring into space for a moment, "well, it's as if the tables have turned. I—don't know how it happened, but I'm the one who's being manipulated, tormented, pushed around. He's rude and inconsiderate —and yet he can be awfully sweet, too, when he likes."

Penny said slowly, her hand on Pam's shoulder, her voice troubled, "I don't like him, Pam."

Pam's lips twisted. "You must be about the only girl around who doesn't," she said. "Marylou, Fran Drake, Tip Flanders—they were all dying to have him ask them to the dance tonight. But I was the one he asked—only—now that he's mad at me, I don't know how it stands. I suppose it's all off."

"It's mean of him to leave you up in the air," Penny said sympathetically. Then, after a thoughtful moment, she asked, "Is that why you've gone overboard for him, because so many others want him?"

Pam frowned. "Of course not. Don't be silly."

A faint smile touched Penny's lips. "Once, when we were talking about Mike, you said that when you got a boy all sewed up, you began to lose interest, that it was when they were hard to get that you found them irresistible."

Color flamed in Pam's face. "That was pretty infantile of me. I'm past that stage now, believe me. I know what I want."

"And Cade Venner's it?" Penny asked. "With all his moods and rages, his lack of consideration, his—" she groped for the right word, "his ugliness of outlook?"

Pam stared at her. "It isn't like you to talk so cruelly about anyone. You don't understand Cade. He went through a lot, in the Marines at eighteen—all that fighting."

Penny's chin was stubborn. She said, "Other fellows have gone through it and it hasn't put them into an emotional tailspin. Jeff Moore saw a lot of active service, too. Mike says he's got a scar on his back six inches long, from a bayonet wound. But Jeff's not like Cade, bitter and mean, distrusting everyone."

"He's not half so attractive, either," Pam said.

"That's a matter of opinion," Penny argued.

"Oh, Pen, don't be silly," Pam said. "That big farmer—how can you even compare him with someone like Cade, who's so handsome that all the girls are gone on him—" her voice broke. Pain and disappointment welled up in her at the thought of all the lovely plans for the dance tonight being washed up, leaving her high and dry.

Penny said earnestly, "Pam, I don't think he's good for you. I wish you wouldn't concentrate on him so much. You never used to let one man monopolize your time."

"I played it smart, didn't I?" Pam murmured. "Had a lot of fun, a lot of laughs. I guess, though," she added, her mouth twisting, "you needn't worry about me seeing too much of Cade any more. He hasn't made the slightest effort to get in touch with me for days. Maybe he never will," she finished starkly.

"Pam," Penny's tone was gentle, "it's no use sitting here brooding. Come on to the game with Mike and me."

"And see Harwood get the tar beaten out of them?" Pam asked, her tone an unconscious echo of Cade's amused derision.

Penny said, frowning, "So maybe we'll get beaten, maybe we won't. You never used to be this way, Pam, supercilious, bored. He's made you that way, he and that super-smooth crowd you run around with. I don't like them and I don't like their effect on you. Please come with us."

Refusal rose to Pam's lips. But then she thought, Why not? After all, it would be more fun than just hanging around the dorm, waiting without much hope for Cade to call. She'd had just about as much of that as she could take. And maybe, if she went out, she might encounter Cade somewhere on the campus. Hope flickered anew at the thought.

"All right," she said suddenly. "If you don't think Mike will mind."

15

A Date for the Dance

THE day was crisp and sunny, with a sharp enlivening nip in the air, perfect football weather. The stands were filling up fast and the crowd spoke and laughed and screeched all about as Penny and Pam and Mike found their seats and settled into them. The gayety and enthusiasm were contagious. Pam felt her spirits lift as she looked about. The breeze whipped fresh color into her cheeks and tossed her dark hair. It seemed, after her doldrums of the past few days, as if she had been lost in some dank cave and had only now found her way out into the sunshine. She tried to put the thought of Cade Venner entirely from her, but it was still there, a dull ache under the thin veneer of carefree happiness.

Mike said, "Boy, we must have been living right! Weather like this for the Homecoming game."

Usually Mike worked on Saturdays in the school bookstore, but everyone had time off today. Mike waited tables in the senior dorm, too. As usual, he had as many jobs as

123

he could handle. But he was doing well with his studies, despite all his jobs. And, just as it had been back at Glen High, everyone liked him. He was one of the freshmen recently elected to the Student Council, which was quite an honor. Pam could see Penny's quiet pride in him shining from her gray eyes as people all about hailed him and he called good-naturedly back to them.

Pam felt rather proud of him herself, she realized. No longer was there the slightest undercurrent of jealousy in her feeling toward Penny. Pam liked Mike as well as ever, but there was a difference in her liking. She really felt toward him now as she supposed she might have felt toward a brother if she had had one. The easy friendship and camaraderie between them carried no slightest echo of the old personal attraction he had once exerted for her, however unintentionally.

"Hey, there's Jeff!" Mike exclaimed suddenly.

And Pam, following the direction of his glance, saw Jeff Moore's tall, easy-moving figure ascending the steps of the grandstand. Mike called to him and stood up, waving and beckoning. Jeff waved back and moved on toward them, grinning.

"We can squeeze him in, can't we?" Mike said, sliding closer to Penny.

And Penny said, "Of course," with equal enthusiasm.

Which left Pam with little choice other than to slide over, too, making room for Jeff beside her.

"Hi, characters," Jeff greeted them all. "Never thought I'd make it. I'm a fugitive from a mess of fence-mending, but I couldn't miss the Homecoming game."

The band came marching onto the field then, resplendent in their red and white uniforms, trumpets blaring, drums booming, and Pam felt herself caught up in the general enthusiasm and excitement. But a part of her seemed to stand aside, scoffing, as Cade would have scoffed. Where was he, Pam wondered? Even as she watched the game and talked and laughed with Penny and Mike and Jeff, her glance darted off frequently to search the stand on the off-chance that Cade might have come. But there was no sign of him, although she did see Tip Flanders' flaming red head and Marylou Ritter's blond one. Tip was with Terry Morris and Marylou with Bill Heath, all members of Pam's special crowd. She felt a faint embarrassment when they looked her way and waved, knowing that they would be amused to see her with Jeff Moore. If they told Cade, he would be amused, too, Pam supposed. Or he might be angry. Cade didn't like Jeff and Pam had a suspicion that the animosity was mutual. She didn't think there was, actually, anything at the root of it beyond the natural clash of their personalities, which were so completely different.

After awhile Jeff said, his tone quietly amused, "Somehow I have the feeling you haven't got your mind on the game."

"Oh, sure, I have," Pam denied. "The score's thirteen to seven, their favor. And it's the first quarter of the last half and—"

"Okay, okay, you've convinced me." Jeff chuckled. "You just kept sort of looking around, as if you were expecting to see someone."

"I'm seeing a lot of people," Pam said airily, implying that she wasn't looking for anyone special. "There are more people here than I've ever seen at a Harwood game."

"Homecoming's big stuff," Jeff grinned. But there was

no hint of superiority in his attitude. "The game, the bonfire last night, the big dance."

Pam nodded. "Yes, I know." She turned her glance squarely toward Jeff, asking, "I suppose you find it all rather childish and amusing?"

"Why should I?" Jeff inquired.

"Oh, being a bit older," Pam said, "having been in service and all."

"I'm not that old." Jeff chuckled. "If I'd gone straight into college out of high school, I'd probably have been a senior by this time instead of a freshman. But I reckon I'd still have enjoyed a good football game."

Pam hadn't thought of it just like that before. Jeff's attitude was altogether different than Cade's. She asked, her face still turned toward him, "Doesn't it seem a little silly to you, though—I mean everyone taking it so seriously and the team with their do-or-die-for-dear-old-Harwood attitude?"

Jeff's hazel eyes were narrowed quizzically, regarding her. "Does it seem silly to you?"

"Well, no," Pam admitted, "but then—"

"Because if it did," Jeff went on, "I'd feel kind of sorry for you. Enthusiasm's a quality it's a shame to lose. It gives things a nice sparkle and makes life a lot more fun. And—" he added, with a little easy shrug of his broad shoulders, "I guess we have to be willing to do-or-die for something. And when you're in college, it might as well be victory in the Homecoming game as anything else."

The cheerleaders went into a series of cart-wheels then and Pam found herself telling Jeff, a little smile curving her mouth, "I used to do that when I was in high school."

"No fooling?" Jeff said. "Cart-wheels and all?"

"Oh, definitely cart-wheels." Pam laughed.

The stands responded loudly to the cheerleaders' commands and gyrations. Pam cheered, too, and watched the game with heightened interest. When Harwood scored a spectacular touchdown a few seconds before the end of the final quarter, she found herself on her feet, gripping Jeff's arm and screaming with the others. When the ball soared between the goal posts for the kick that won the game, Jeff caught her up in a great bear hug and swung her off her feet in a burst of exuberance and elation.

"Boy, oh, boy, what a game!" he exclaimed, grinning down at Pam as he set her on the solid wood of the grandstand once more.

"It was wonderful." Pam laughed up at him.

She felt a little self-conscious, now that the mad frenzy of those last few seconds of play was over. She wondered if Tip or Fran or Marylou had seen her, being hugged like that by Jeff Moore. And would Cade hear that she had been at the game with Jeff, that she had appeared to be having a grand time? It *had* been fun, Pam admitted to herself. She was glad she had let Penny persuade her to come, that Jeff had happened along and had sat with them. She didn't even mind his hugging her like that. His arms had been strong, yet gentle at the same time. Never had Pam felt herself lifted so effortlessly, as if she had been feather-light. It had given her a strange feeling, a sense of being helpless, yet protected, that was rather pleasant. She couldn't quite fathom her own reaction.

But she had little chance to dwell on it. She and Jeff and Penny and Mike made their way down from the grandstand and onto the field, swept along in a shouting, milling, hysterically enthusiastic mob of students and alumni bent on celebrating victory. Over the din, Pam could hear the mellow tone of the Old Hall bell, which sounded only on such special occasions as this. A kind of thickness came up in her throat at the measured chiming. It was a link with the past, Pam thought, and the sense of continuity it signified formed a bridge between the faraway days when the school was first founded and the present. Students in queer old-fashioned clothes had listened to that bell, had been moved by its notes pealing out across the campus, just as she was moved now.

How amused Cade would have been with such thoughts, Pam reflected, a wry smile tugging at her lips.

Jeff told her, pressed close against her in the pushing jubilant throng, "That makes the victory official." And there was something in his tone that made Pam sure the sound of the old bell had touched him, too.

"I know." She nodded. "It's the first time I've ever heard it ring, though."

"Harwood's been taking quite a shellacking this year," Jeff admitted. "That's the way it goes. Next season we'll probably have a winning streak."

"We could use one," Pam said.

By the time they had got out of the thickest of the crowd, they had lost Mike and Penny. After a few minutes of fruitless search, Jeff suggested, "Let's stop by the Union and grab a bite. If we can fight our way in, that is. Penny and Mike will probably be there."

And so would all her closest friends, Pam thought wryly, ensconced as was their inalienable right and custom in the corner booth. Still, she reflected, they'd seen her at the game with Jeff, she might as well carry the situation through with a flourish.

"Okay," she said, smiling up at him, "let's."

The Union was more crowded than Pam had ever seen it. Jeff caught sight of Mike near the soda fountain, and he and Pam moved to join the other couple. From the corner of her eye, Pam saw that Cade wasn't in the usual booth with the rest of the crowd.

So what? she asked herself with a kind of bitter self-derision. She hadn't really thought he would be.

For the next half hour, Pam went through all the motions of a girl having a very enjoyable time in her present company. She seemed her old gay self and she sensed Penny's relief to have her so. Mike, too, looked upon her with beaming approval. She supposed he had been troubled over her close association with Cade Venner, just as Penny had been. Those two usually saw eye to eye on any matter.

During a brief moment of privacy, when Penny and Mike were engaged in conversation with the couple sitting beyond them at the circular counter, Jeff said to Pam, "I suppose you'll be wanting to get back to the dorm before long, so you can get all prettied up for the dance."

Pam said lightly, "I'm not going to the dance. But if you're in a hurry—"

"All I have to rush home to," Jeff admitted, "are some neglected chores. I wasn't figuring on going to the dance, either. But—" he added, a note of surprise in his voice, "I sure thought you'd be going. A popular girl like you."

"Thanks," Pam murmured. "Let's just blame it on a rather involved set of circumstances beyond my control, shall we?"

That covered the situation quite well, she thought. She had turned down several invitations to accept Cade's, then he had let her down and that was that.

" 'The Lord hates a coward,' " Jeff quoted drily. "That used to be one of my grandmother Nesbitt's favorite sayings. Of course," he admitted with a little, not too confident grin, "she also used to say 'Fools rush in where angels fear to tread.' Maybe that's what I'm doing right now, but I'm going to chance it just the same. How about going to the dance with me?"

Pam stared at him for a moment in genuine surprise. She hadn't expected that. Go to the dance with Jeff? She considered thoughtfully for a moment.

"Kind of short notice, I know," Jeff grinned apologetically. "But I figured you'd been invited weeks ago. Otherwise I'd have asked you sooner."

A little smile tugged at one corner of Pam's mouth. She thought, It would serve Cade right if I went with Jeff. Even if he's not there himself, someone will be sure to tell him. And the way he feels about Jeff, he'd be furious.

The thought of Cade, really angry, sent little quivers of excited dread up and down her spine.

Jeff said, "If you're trying to figure out a polite way to say 'no' without hurting my feelings, don't bother. Just let me have it and get it over with. But say something."

Pam stopped struggling with the smile and let it break through. "You know," she said, "I just might take you up on that—if you really mean it."

"Mean it?" Jeff repeated. "You don't think I'd joke about a thing like that! Will you go with me, Pam?"

She nodded and his answering grin was wide and wholehearted. He squeezed her elbow hard.

"Well, glory be!" Jeff said. He leaned over to tell Mike,

"I've got me a date to take Pam to the Homecoming dance."

"Good for you," Mike grinned back at him.

And Penny said, her eyes shining, "Oh, Pam, I'm glad. Shall we all go together?"

"That'd be swell," Mike said.

Jeff's questioning glance came back to Pam. "That okay with you?"

"Of course," she said. "It'll be like old times, double dating with Pen and Mike."

But in her mind's eye she wasn't seeing Jeff's pleased smile at all. She was seeing Cade, darkly scowling . . .

16   *Jeff or Cade?*

"I WISH," Pam mourned, brushing her dark hair with deft swirling strokes, "I'd known a little in advance that I'd be going tonight. My hair's a mess."

"No, it isn't," Penny said. "It looks fine." She came up to Pam then, asking, "Zip me up, will you?"

Pam turned around and did so. She told Penny, "You look wonderful. That shade of yellow's perfect for you."

"You look wonderful, too," Penny said, giving Pam an affectionate little hug. "And dressing in the same room like this—well, it's like being home again, isn't it?"

Pam chuckled. "Crowded, but cozy."

She turned back then to her reflection in the dresser mirror. She could see the fitted bodice of her deep green dress, the beginning of the skirt's fullness, accenting her slim waist, the creamy smoothness of her bare arms and throat and shoulders. Her gray eyes looked back at her rather quizzically and the expression of her mouth, not quite smiling, was faintly amused.

She said, "This is the most cock-eyed, spur-of-the-moment date I've ever had, I think."

132

"I know." Penny nodded. "But considering the way Cade acted, getting mad over nothing and letting you down—well, I think things have really worked out almost better than you could expect."

Pam had to admit that this was so. Still, it seemed queer to her to think of attending the dance with Jeff Moore, after turning down Bill Heath and Terry Morris. But when Bill and Terry had asked her, she had been planning to go with Cade. Oh, well, Pam thought, trying to be philosophical about the situation, Jeff's better than nobody.

A small qualm of inner shame followed in the wake of that unflattering reflection. Jeff was really quite attractive, Pam reminded herself, if you cared for big, easy-moving, drawling types. He was nice and agreeable and dependable. It wasn't his fault he was unable to drive the sardonic dark image of Cade Venner from her mind and heart. It was unreasonable to expect him to, when she was so obsessed with Cade.

In almost every room in the dormitory, girls were getting ready for the dance, chattering and laughing in high-pitched tones, running back and forth in very scanty array to borrow nail polish or jewelry, to beg for help with recalcitrant fasteners, to ask advice on which accessory did the most for their ensembles. Excitement and anticipation were like an electric storm in the charged atmosphere. The Homecoming Dance was one of the big festivities of the year, with all the college clubs combining to sponsor it. Penny had worked on the decorations, helping to transform the big gym into a red and white wonderland, which created the impression that the dancers would be moving under a giant striped canopy, held up by red and white poles like great peppermint sticks. Pam had been on the floor-show committee and she knew that quite an array of talent had been rounded up. It was going to be such fun!

She said to Penny, with a little laugh, "Wouldn't it be ghastly if Jeff turned up in that awful old truck he sometimes drives back and forth?"

"He won't," Penny said, giving Pam a slightly reproving look. "He's got a perfectly good sedan, or his family has. Anyway, we'll all be walking. It's only a step to the gym."

"I know," Pam said. "I was just fooling."

And she had been. Still a queer stifled feeling of foreboding seemed to lie heavily upon her, a hunch that something was going to go wrong about the evening, although she couldn't imagine what. She wasn't, actually, worried about Jeff. He was perfectly presentable and his manners were good. Just because she had originally planned to go to the dance with Cade, whom she found so much more attractive, was no reason to sell Jeff short. Then what was she worried about, Pam asked herself, and couldn't find an answer.

Around nine o'clock, escorts began arriving. The rumble of male voices ascended from the lounge downstairs and the girls who weren't going to the dance were kept busy running back and forth from their vantage point at the head of the stairs to relay the word of which girl's date was waiting for her. The halls echoed with calls of, "Oh, Jane—Curt's here," "Sue, Hank's been waiting ages! Better step on it," and the like.

Then Pam heard her own name called, but the message

that followed it struck her with startling impact. "Pam—
oh, Pam, Cade's here."

Pam stood perfectly still, staring at Penny. "Cade?" her
lips formed the word almost soundlessly.

Penny said, her eyes flashing, "The nerve of him, just
turning up like this without a word! What are you going
to do?"

"That's a good question," Pam muttered automatically, her thoughts rushing off at crazy tangents, her heart
hammering under her ribs. She told Penny, "I'll have to
go down and talk to him—try to straighten it out. Oh,
what a mess!"

"Pam!" Penny caught her wrists as she moved toward
the door, swung her around to look into her face. "You
wouldn't go with him after the way he's acted?"

Pam pulled away from her. "I don't know," she said in
a queer strained tone. "How do I know what I'll do till I
see him, talk with him?"

Excitement exploded in her at the thought of Cade
downstairs, waiting for her. Her lips felt dry and she ran
her tongue along them. Her blood seemed to race
through her veins in a throbbing, heavy surge.

Penny said accusingly, "Pam, Jeff and Mike will be here
any minute. You can't just stand Jeff up."

"Let me alone!" Pam cried. She caught up her coat and
left, calling back to Penny from the doorway, "I'll work
it out."

I'll work it out, she repeated to herself as she made her
way through the confusion and congestion of the corridor,
the stairs. People spoke to her and she answered, but her
thoughts milled in futile circles all the while, so that she

had no idea what was said, or what she replied. Oh, what a mess! her thoughts exclaimed over and over. She had told Cade she'd go with him, she'd accepted his invitation weeks ago. But when he left her in such a towering rage and didn't phone or come near her—well, naturally she had supposed their date was off. And now, here she was, committed to go with Jeff, but with Cade downstairs waiting for her.

He was standing just inside the lounge, Pam saw as she entered the big crowded room, one shoulder leaned against the wall, dark and disturbingly handsome in his formal clothes. He had a carnation in his button-hole, a cellophane box with an orchid in it under his elbow. He turned his head and saw her and a pleased smile drew his lips back from his strong white teeth.

"Hi, gorgeous," he said in a low, intimate tone, his dark glance boldly admiring.

His arrogance, his apparent assumption that he had the situation completely in hand, infuriated Pam. A second before she hadn't been sure what she'd say to him.

Now the words that came through her lips in a low, angry tone, were, "What are you doing here?"

Cade's thick black brows rose inquiringly. "What am I doing?" he repeated. "Why, calling for my girl, of course."

No one was paying any particular attention to them, although people kept passing close by. The occupants of the big room shifted and changed, arrived and left, intent on their own affairs.

Pam's gray eyes were stormy. "And I suppose you thought I'd just be waiting around to see whether you decided to turn up or not!"

"Well," Cade appeared to consider the matter, his voice easy and good-natured, "I guess you haven't exactly been waiting around. I hear you went to the game today with Jeff Moore."

Despite the casual tone, something of tenseness, some hint of curbed resentment in his manner, gave Pam the key to the situation. Someone had told Cade of seeing her with Jeff, whom he disliked so intensely. His own imagination had probably led him to suspect she might be planning to go with Jeff to the dance as well.

Pam glared at Cade, accusing, "So you figured I might not sit around moping tonight, just because you let me down, and that you'd better turn up as though nothing had happened!"

His eyes told her that she had hit on the truth. But he lifted his shoulders in a little shrug, saying, "Ah, don't be like that, baby. We had a date, didn't we? Why wouldn't I come?"

He extended the orchid in its transparent box toward her ingratiatingly. But Pam wasn't looking anywhere except upward into his face. And she steeled her heart against his charm.

She said, her voice still low so that the others all around wouldn't hear, but crackling with anger just the same, "You wouldn't come for the same reason you haven't come near me or phoned for days! And you didn't even have any excuse to be mad!"

"Who's mad?" Cade asked, grinning down at her.

"I am," Pam said, although something warm and weak within her tried to respond to his smile, his coaxing manner. Pam thought: I must be crazy, still feeling like this toward him after the way he's acted, still wanting to go with him in spite of everything.

She clenched her hands hard at her sides, where they were hidden by the crisp fullness of her dress, willing herself to hold out, afraid she couldn't.

"Not any more, are you?" Cade coaxed, his voice low, husky, breaking up her anger into bits and pieces that Pam sought frantically to put back together. "Not if I'm sorry?"

Pam drew a deep, shaken breath. She wished she could withdraw her eyes from his, but it was as though she were drowning in the dark intensity of his glance.

And then a voice spoke behind her, a masculine voice, slow and rather drawling, but with a quiet positiveness and strength in it. "Hi, Pam," Jeff Moore said. "Hope I didn't keep you waiting."

Pam wasn't quite sure whether the indrawn breath she heard was Cade's or her own. She turned her head toward Jeff, smiling with not too steady lips. Behind him she saw Penny and Mike. And Penny's eyes were anxious and Mike's jaw rather grim.

Pam said, "Hi, Jeff," and felt new strength flow into her. It was as though he were a rock, close there beside her, something to cling to so that the dark current pulling her toward Cade, toward the weakness of capitulation, could not overpower her. She said, "You're not late—not really."

Above her head, she saw Cade's glance lock with Jeff's. And sheer hate looked out of Cade's eyes and Jeff's solid jaw grew even more firm, although no word passed between them.

Pam said, her voice low, but firm, her eyes on Cade's

face. "I'm going with Jeff, Cade. You should have known I would after—everything."

Cade's eyes were narrow dark slits looking down at her and she could see a muscle tense along the angle of his cheek as his teeth bit hard together. But all he said, to Pam alone, ignoring the others, was, "As you say."

Then he walked away from them, out of the lounge, and Pam caught her trembling lip hard between her teeth. "Well—that's that," she said huskily.

She felt Penny's arm, firm and approving, about her waist. It helped a little to curb the sense of desolation and loss that washed over her. But it didn't help very much, nor did the voices of Penny and Mike and Jeff, trying to smooth the situation over and drive Cade from her thoughts, trying to make her feel right again.

But would she ever feel right again, Pam wondered? With Cade gone from her like that, with this bitter ache of emptiness within her? And yet she had done what she had known she should, what all the dictates of decency and conscience told her was her only course. She couldn't go running off with Cade after the way he'd treated her, after promising Jeff she'd go with him. There was such a thing as pride, Pam thought, her chin lifting.

Jeff held her coat for her and she slipped her arms into it. She accepted the corsage of yellow rosebuds he handed her and exclaimed over it and thanked him. Then she went out with Penny and Mike and him into the clear cool night. Their conversation wasn't exactly effervescent, but it was adequate. And Pam was grateful for the casual talk, the efforts of the others to help smooth over the jagged edges of the scene with Cade which had held a threat of ugly violence. Pam had been afraid for a shaken moment that Cade was going to strike Jeff and the thought of the effect of such an action there in the crowded festive lounge had sickened her.

As they walked down the wide path toward the sidewalk, Pam saw a cellophane box, with its fragile contents, crushed almost beyond recognition on the white gravel. But Jeff brushed the ruin aside with his foot and none of them mentioned it.

17 *A Dance and a Picnic*

THE Homecoming Dance, the first big dance the twins had attended at college, was always to remain somewhat vague in Pam's memory. It was like a dance in a dream, with a misty unreality about it, although the music was real enough, and the various partners with whom she danced, and the dazzling red and white decorations. Pam's feet followed the rhythms of the big name band with the ease of long practice. Pam's lips murmured just the right gay words to keep her partners amused and interested and coming back for more. But it was as though only a part of her did these things, while the other part stood aside and looked on it all as a spectator, having no immediate share in the proceedings. This other self mourned, sure that by her actions tonight she had lost all chance of winning Cade back. His arrogance wouldn't countenance her decision to go with Jeff rather than him. He'd probably never speak to her again. No more would she sit with Cade in the corner booth at the

Union, their shoulders touching chummily, knowing the warm, excited thrill of his mere presence. No more for her the quick pride of seeing herself envied by the other girls in her crowd because of Cade's preference.

Where was he now, Pam wondered desolately. Not here at any rate. Unobtrusively, her glance would check the stag line, hoping to catch a glimpse of him. But then she would tip her head back and smile up at her partner and answer what was said to her and go through all the motions of having a wonderful time. Pam knew the motions so well she never faltered.

Rather to her surprise, Jeff proved to be an excellent dancer. Even better than Cade, she had to admit. Jeff's arm was firm and sure around her waist, but not too firm. She followed his lead easily, since his touch was not so unsettling as she found Cade's.

"Having fun?" he asked once, his hazel eyes looking directly into hers.

"Of course," Pam told him, and meant it.

"Not worrying about Dreamboat?" He grinned. "I guess he decided to give the dance a miss."

"Let's not even talk about him," Pam said. But her glance dropped away from Jeff's and she felt resentment rise in her. She'd come to the dance with him, she thought. Couldn't he be satisfied with that and let well enough alone?

"Okay with me," Jeff said mildly.

During an intermission Pam encountered Tip Flanders in the powder room. They stood side by side at the long mirror repairing their make-up and Tip asked, her brown eyes under her flaming curly bangs avid with interest, "Darling, I've been dying to ask you! I thought you were coming with Cade, but I heard you'd had a big bust-up. Then, when he turned up at the dorm tonight, I figured you'd got back together. But now you're with Jeff Moore and Cade didn't even come and what happened? We're all popping with curiosity!"

"Nothing happened," Pam said, her glance meeting Tip's in the mirror. "I had a date with Cade for the dance, then when he got mad over nothing, I figured it was off. So I told Jeff I'd come with him. Then Cade did an about-face and called for me tonight as though everything was all set."

"And you stood Cade up?" Tip asked incredulously, her brows rising.

"I wouldn't call it that," Pam said in sharp annoyance, "after the way he acted—"

"Pet," Tip told her, "we just don't see eye to eye, I'm afraid. However Cade acted, I'm just the type that would come running if he lifted a beckoning finger. He's so darned attractive—and, after all, you did have a date with him."

"I had a date with Jeff, too," Pam pointed out. "And it certainly wouldn't be very ethical to break it just because of Cade's sudden whim."

Tip shrugged, a slight gesture which, coupled with her quizzical smile, said as plainly as words could have, "Of course, it's your own affair, but I think you're quite mad."

Pam turned back to brush on more lip-stick with a hand that wasn't entirely steady. Tip's opinion, she had an idea, would be shared rather generally by the rest of the girls in her crowd. In fact, there was one part of Pam that agreed with it, too . . .

Later that night, after a stop at the Union for hamburgers and a slow walk back to Grace Kirkland, Penny and Mike and Pam and Jeff lingered on the steps, talking. They were not alone. The steps were crowded with other lingerers, the soft colors of the girls' formal dresses pale and ghostly in the moonlight, the men's clothes making a darker accent. Everyone hated to end the evening, to go in, although only a few minutes more remained until the hour that had been set as the deadline. Mike's arm was around Penny. Jeff's arm was through Pam's. Their voices added to the faint murmur of voices all about.

Jeff said, his eye on the moon, "Clear day tomorrow, it looks like."

"Say!" Mike exclaimed. "Why don't we have a picnic?"

"You and your boy scout instincts," Pam said.

But Penny agreed, "Let's! We've been wanting to for ages and this fall weather's so perfect."

"Why don't I come by for you tomorrow and drive you out to the farm?" Jeff took it up. "Lots of good picnic spots around there."

"Oh, Pam, what fun!" Penny said enthusiastically. "You will, won't you?"

"Why—I guess so," Pam said.

There had been, it seemed, no valid reason for refusing. And when the next day proved to be one of those perfect fall days when the season appeared to be looking backward coquettishly over its shoulder at the vanishing back of summer, Pam was glad she had agreed. After chapel she and Penny got permission to pack a picnic basket of sandwiches and fruit and cookies in the dormitory kitchen. Then they donned blue jeans and plaid flannel shirts and tied scarves gypsy-fashion around their hair.

Mike and Jeff called for them at a little before noon.

Since Pam and Penny and Mike had car-riding privileges, which had had to be signed for by their parents, and since Jeff, living off campus, had special permission to drive, no rules were being broken by their trip in Jeff's sedan.

Penny exclaimed, laughing, "I haven't been in a car for so long, I actually get a kick out of it."

Pam nodded in agreement. But it wasn't because she hadn't had plenty of opportunity, she thought. So far, she had managed to avoid riding in Cade's big gray and red convertible when they had gone by bus into Cleveland to a show, or dancing. Nor was Cade the only one in their special crowd who had secret arrangements for keeping a car in some city garage and using it for off-campus dates. Pam had had to take a good deal of kidding for her determination not to break school rules, when there was such small chance of being caught.

Jeff said, "I'm sorry my folks won't be home today. I'd like you to meet them. But they drove over to Fairview to see my married sister."

"Maybe you wanted to go with them," Pam said.

But Jeff shook his head. "Somebody had to feed the stock. Besides, I like picnics."

They drove along, not taking the highway, but following less used roads that curved around clumps of flaming sumac and white birch. They passed neatly painted farmhouses with great red barns dwarfing them, saw cattle grazing, red-brown and sleek against the fading green of the fenced fields. There was a kind of quiet peace about the day, the frost-touched countryside, that was at once soothing and uplifting. Pam felt Cade slipping from her thoughts and made no effort to keep him uppermost in her mind. She would enjoy this day, the company of Jeff and Penny and Mike, and get back to the problem of Cade later if she must.

Maybe, Pam thought, I won't have to, maybe I'm free of him, after the hateful way he's acted. Maybe whatever it was that drew me to him is past and done with.

But in her heart she knew this wasn't so . . .

It was a day like many others Pam had spent and yet, in some subtle, not easily identified way, different. Sprawled on a grassy knoll, looking out over a tumbling little creek and the trim pattern of plowed fields stretching off into the distance, they ate their picnic lunch and drank the cold drinks the boys had bought. And they talked and laughed and were companionably silent as the spirit moved them. Penny and Mike sat braced against a sloping tree-trunk, Mike's arm around Penny and her head on his shoulder. But now Pam felt no trace of resentment, of jealousy, as she had that day she had picnicked with Randy and Mike and Penny. Randy, she reflected. His letter yesterday had been the first in weeks. Neither of them wrote very often. He was busy, Pam supposed, as she had been. Maybe he had met someone else who attracted him. She rather hoped he had.

Jeff reached over and tickled the back of her hand with a long twig, bringing her back to the present. He leaned on his elbows, grinning up at her and Pam found her eyes lingering on his face, noting the look of strength about it, liking the steady way his hazel eyes looked into hers.

She asked, smiling a little, "Is all this land yours, this where we're picnicking and over there, those plowed fields beyond the brook?"

"It's my father's," Jeff told her, "three hundred and

sixty acres of it. Someday it'll go to us kids, my brother and two sisters and me."

Pam asked him, "Have you always lived here?" Over to the left a considerable distance off she could see the red roof of the farmhouse Jeff had told her was his home, the great barn on beyond it.

Jeff nodded. "Always, except when I was away in the army. My father was born here, too."

"And you like farming?" Pam asked. "You'd be satisfied to stay on here?"

"Why not?" Jeff grinned. He turned over on his back then and lay there, staring up at the blue sky with the little soft-looking clouds drifting lazily across it. "You know of a better way of life? I don't and I've seen plenty of different ones while I was away. I've dreamed about this place on stinking little islands in the Pacific and in great big cities right here in the United States. You couldn't give me city life or a desk job. This is where I belong and I know it."

"Why do you bother with college then?" Pam asked.

Jeff told her, "You've got some kind of a cock-eyed city notion about farmers. You'll have to meet my folks, so you can see how mistaken you are. My mother and father both went to college and they mean to give us kids the same privilege, if we care to take it. Harwood's got a good agricultural course, and I'll take some of the subjects that are tied in with farming. But there's nothing wrong with a farmer knowing a little something about mathematics and literature and such, too. You should see my dad's library. I haven't even read all the books in it yet and I started young, too."

Penny and Mike entered into the conversation then and, by the time they had all finished discussing the subject, Pam felt she knew quite a lot more about modern farms and farmers than she had before. She also felt considerably better acquainted with Jeff himself. And she liked what she learned about him and felt a new respect for him growing within her. There seemed to be a lot more to Jeff than she had supposed. She doubted if she would ever think of him again as "that big farmer." He might be that, but he was other things as well.

When the shadows began to lengthen, Jeff rose to his feet. "I've got some chores to do." He grinned down at the others. "You can hike around and explore, or wait for me here. Or," he added, "you can come along with me, if you like. It might be kind of novel for a bunch of city slickers like you."

"Are we going to let him get away with such insults?" Mike demanded, getting to his feet.

Pam and Penny followed suit and the four of them hiked across rolling fields and little gullies until they reached the great red barn. The house beyond it was tall and old-fashioned in architecture, but so well kept up, with its white painted siding and dark green shutters, that its age didn't seem to matter, except to impart an effect of roomy comfort.

Jeff led the way into the barn, switched on lights to dispel the shadowy gloom. It was clean and well-ordered, smelling not at all unpleasantly of hay and animals. Tractors and other pieces of farm equipment, at the uses of which the twins and even Mike could only guess, were lined up at one side. Pam and Penny wandered around examining them while Mike helped Jeff with his chores.

Then, as cattle congregated in the barnyard, lowing plaintively as they waited to be fed and watered and milked, the twins went out and leaned on the fence to observe the animals and enjoy the novelty of it all.

When Jeff was through with his work, they all walked back in the gathering dusk to where they had left the car near their picnic site.

"Hasn't this been fun?" Penny exclaimed.

And Pam nodded. She had come on the picnic with no particular enthusiasm, simply because it afforded a way to spend an otherwise empty day. But she had enjoyed herself more than she had expected to. Something of the quiet tranquillity of the bright fall day seemed to have entered into her spirit, driving out the tension and unhappiness her difficulties with Cade had engendered. In fact, she realized now with some surprise, Cade had been absent from her thoughts for a much longer period than usual.

The four of them drove back to Harwood, stopping en route at a little diner for hamburgers and French fries and thick mugs of warming, delicious coffee. In front of Grace Kirkland they sat for awhile in Jeff's car, talking, then said good-night. Pam and Penny went up the steps to the entrance arm in arm, as Mike and Jeff drove off.

"It's been a grand day," Pam said.

"Hasn't it?" Penny agreed, yawning. "I'm sleepy, though. All that fresh air."

They opened the door and went inside. Marylou Ritter was crossing the hall toward the lounge and she glanced up at the twins' entrance.

"Well, hi, you two," she greeted them. "Where have you been all day?"

"Picnicking," Pam said. "Why, did you miss us?"

"Somebody did," Marylou said drily. "Or at least, he must have missed you."

"He?" Pam's tone was questioning, but sudden awareness broke over her as to just who Marylou meant.

"Cade," her friend informed her with a little, knowing smile. "He's been burning up the telephone wires all day. If he called once, he must have called five times."

Pam's heart quickened and happiness flowed through her in a rich tide. "Well, what do you know?" she murmured.

18   *Thanksgiving*

Now that she and Cade had made up again, the days seemed to overflow for Pam with a rich, sweet tide of delight, of satisfaction. Life followed a stimulating pattern, hard work on her studies, followed by the relaxation of fun and dates. She took a good deal of kidding from Cade over her efforts to keep her grades up. But she made the effort just the same and took the kidding in her stride.

"It's different for you," she told him. "Nobody's having to work hard to keep you in college. But even so—" she broke off, knowing Cade wouldn't like what she had been about to add.

"Even so what?" Cade asked, lifting a quizzical eyebrow.

"I was just going to say," Pam admitted, "that I should think you'd get some personal satisfaction out of accomplishing something at college, not just wasting your time."

"Please," Cade lifted a reproving hand, "no lectures.

It's my time and if I prefer to waste it, that's my business."

But his tone remained casual, unruffled. He wasn't so prone to fly into unreasonable rages these days. His increased amiability, Pam realized, seemed to have stemmed from the night she had gone to the dance with Jeff. Was it caused, she wondered, by Cade's realization that he couldn't push her around as freely as he had supposed, that there was a point at which she wouldn't take any more? Or was the change in him due merely to the fact that he disliked Jeff too intensely to let him win over a girl in whom he, Cade, was still interested? Whatever the cause, the results were highly satisfactory from Pam's viewpoint. She had had more dates than ever with Cade during the past few weeks. And her friends were outspoken in their envy.

Cade wasn't content with the unimpressive opportunities for amusement offered by the small, sleepy town of Harwood. Movies, bowling and the like might suffice for Pam's occasional dates with Jeff. But scarcely a Saturday night passed that she and Cade didn't take the bus in to Cleveland, to have dinner, or see a show, or dance at some night club, indulging in all the glittery glamorous excitement that Pam loved. Sometimes they went alone, sometimes with other couples. And always Cade tried to beguile her into driving somewhere in his convertible. But Pam had managed so far to resist the lure of the forbidden and hold out for taxis to their destination.

Once Cade demanded, "What are you, chicken? Who'd ever know anything about it at school?"

But Pam said good-naturedly, "Maybe I am, at that.

It just seems sort of silly to me to break a rule for kicks. And particularly a rule they're so fussy about."

"They're fussy about all their silly rules," Cade argued. Still, Pam stuck to her guns.

Almost before Pam and Penny realized it, Thanksgiving was upon them. The short holiday didn't allow them enough time to go home and so, along with a lot of others, they stayed on at school. Cade flew back to St. Louis, expense being of small importance to him. And Pam anticipated a rather lonely week-end without him. But Jeff Moore surprised her by inviting her, along with Penny and Mike, to spend Thanksgiving Day at the farm.

"I've been wanting you to meet my family," he told Pam. "And this seems a made-to-order opportunity."

Pam didn't think she'd ever forget the friendliness and warmth of that day with the Moores. The big old farmhouse proved to be even more comfortable and homelike inside than its exterior had appeared to Pam that day of the picnic when she first saw it. The holiday table was loaded with marvelous, hearty country food. And Jeff's parents, his brother and sisters, did their best to make the visitors feel welcome and at ease.

Pam liked the Moores. She found them interesting and congenial, rather to her secret surprise. Maybe, she decided, Jeff had been right when he accused her of having mistaken city notions about farmers. Certainly Mr. Moore's library would have done credit to a professor, yet, according to his own dry words, his specialty was Poland China hogs, while books were just his hobby. Jeff's pleasant, prematurely white-haired mother was charming and alert, active in the nearby town's civic affairs and a witty conversationalist. His pretty married sister and her good-humored young husband were renting an apartment in a small city some forty miles away while they saved their money to buy a farm of their own. And Jeff's younger brother and sister were lively, agreeable children.

The farmhouse had every convenience anyone could want. The cheerful kitchen was equipped with a big electric stove and a gleaming white refrigerator. The furnishings were old, but in good taste, some of them valuable antiques.

"Wouldn't Mother drool over this highboy?" Pam asked Penny, as they were getting into their wraps to go back to school.

Mrs. Moore laid her hand affectionately on the softly glowing wood. "It's cherry," she told them. "And so's the four-poster. My grandparents brought them from New York State in a covered wagon, wrapped in thick quilts to keep from marring the finish. I've often heard my grandmother talk of that trip." She reminisced for a few minutes longer, then finished by telling the twins, "If your mother likes antiques, bring her out here when she visits you at school. I've got lots of things I'd like to show her."

And Pam and Penny promised to do so.

When Cade learned of the way Pam had spent the holiday, he scoffed, "I suppose it's all right if you like to hobnob with a bunch of hicks."

"They're not!" Pam denied hotly. "They're wonderful people, intelligent and friendly. You're just being narrowminded to talk that way!"

Cade chuckled. "When you get mad your eyes turn green. I never noticed that before."

Pam had to laugh with him. There had been a time when her defense of the Moores would have roused his anger. But something had changed Cade. She hoped it lasted . . .

Gran had sent the twins a big box of cookies, so they were having a late evening party for their closest friends in Penny's bedroom. Girls in pajamas and robes and slippers, in pin curls and towel turbans, were sitting on the bed, the chair, the window-seat and floor. Outside in the darkness snow swirled, but inside it was warm and cozy and the chatter and laughter mounted to a crescendo as the hour for Lights Out drew near.

As usual, the talk was mostly of men and dates. Then they got around to a discussion of the showboat, which the college operated in the summer under the sponsorship of the speech and drama department.

"I think it'll be simply out of this world!" Tip Flanders, who was planning to take the course, exclaimed with enthusiasm. "Imagine, a regular showboat, and we'll be giving performances in all those cute old river towns. And old-time melodramas must be loads of fun to do. You can be so hammy."

Pam nodded. "It does sound like fun. Of course, they tell me there's work involved, too. Deck-swabbing and kitchen police and shifting scenery and the like. But even so, it would be quite an experience."

There was a wistful note in her voice. The circumstances that made it impossible for her and Penny to take a summer course remained unchanged. It wouldn't be fair to Mother, even aside from the money that would be required. Pam felt a twinge of regret as the interesting discussion continued. Several others present beside Tip were planning to enroll for the showboat course.

"Mike may get a job helping run the tug that pulls it," Penny said.

And Pam knew, just from Penny's tone, that she, too, was secretly sorry they would be left out of it all. But they couldn't let Mother down and leave her to spend a lonely summer without them. There was just no use in even thinking about the showboat.

That, however, was more easily decided than done. And when, a week or so later, Mike told them that his summer job as helper to Captain Anderson was all set, Pam knew that Penny, despite her show of pleasure for Mike's sake, must be feeling a little glum inside.

Mike himself said, "I don't like the idea of spending most of the summer away from Glenhurst. But, gee, Pen, it's such a good job. And I figure, if I'm ever going to be a writer, I ought to take advantage of any unusual sort of job that will give me a chance to have different experiences."

"Of course, you should," Penny said staunchly. "I think it's a wonderful chance for you, Mike."

"I wish you could go," Mike said.

"Maybe," Pam heard herself saying, "if I stayed home and helped Mother and if Howard House has been doing awfully well, you could go, Pen."

Penny slipped her arm around Pam, gave her a little affectionate hug. "Now wouldn't that be crazy? If one of us could go, it should be you, not me. You're the actress in our family. I might be all right on kitchen police and costume mending. But anyway, it's a nice thought and I appreciate it."

There was a lot to think about those days besides the showboat. Most of the talk around campus was of the Christmas holidays looming ahead. But there was much studying to be done first. Mid-semester exams, scheduled for late January, were already beginning to cast their warning shadows before them. Pam had been keeping her work up quite well, despite Cade's amused ridicule.

When he scoffed, "Getting to be a regular grind, aren't you?" Pam said lightly, "Oh, nothing like that. But if I'm going to college at all, I don't want to stay a freshman forever."

Cade shrugged. "Somehow, I can't get vitally concerned about it. If I flunk out, my old man will fix me up somewhere else, where the requirements aren't so stiff. He wouldn't want me hanging around underfoot at home any more than I'd want to hang around."

Pam said, feeling a little surge of pity for him, sensing the lack of something fundamental in his home background, "Cade, wouldn't you like to get decent grades for your own sake, just to prove to yourself that you could?"

"Why?" Cade drawled.

Pam felt herself coloring under the sardonic amusement in his dark glance, yet something inside drove her to persist. "I should think, for the sake of your own self-respect—"

"Don't go noble on me," Cade growled. "I have a perfectly healthy self-respect as it is. I think I'm quite a guy, frankly. Don't you?"

Pam had to laugh, admitting, "Well, yes. But I could be prejudiced."

"Just keep on that way," Cade told her . . .

19   *Home for the Holidays*

THE weeks before the Christmas holidays passed slowly, but at last they were over. Back at home, it seemed incredible that three months had elapsed since the twins had slept in these familiar maple beds, had wakened to bright winter sunshine filtering in between plaid gingham curtains.

It's as if we hadn't been away at all, Pam reflected wonderingly on their first morning back. She lay there in that first moment of full awakening, her glance skipping fondly about. The pleasant room seemed to have reached out and enfolded her again, just as Mother had held her close for a moment last night after their arrival.

There had been quite a crowd for dinner, Gran and Lucius, looking fit and hearty after their Caribbean cruise in November, Ty Shelton, Celia and the twins. And everyone had had so much to tell, so many questions to ask, that they had lingered long at the table, talking and laughing. It had been like old times, Pam and Penny had agreed, going to bed when it was quite late. They had been too sleepy then to talk much. But they had agreed that Mother had never looked more wonderful. Her blue eyes had glowed when she smiled at them and her dress of soft rose wool had made her look even younger than they remembered.

"Wouldn't it be something," Penny's voice broke into Pam's thoughts, "if Mother and Ty fell in love?"

Pam laughed, turning over on her stomach to contemplate her twin. "Mind reader! I was thinking exactly the same thing. They're on such nice easy terms with each other, and being associated in business and all. And Mother seemed so happy last night."

"That might have been because we were home. But just the same—" Penny's voice trailed off.

"You wish they would get married?" Pam finished for her.

Penny nodded, her eyes shining.

And Pam admitted, "I feel the same way about it."

"Do you, Pam?" There was a happy little note in Penny's voice. "I wasn't sure you would. When she seemed to be getting interested in Paul Gerard, you weren't very keen on it."

"I know, but Ty's different," Pam said. "He's not foot-loose like Paul. He'd make a better husband, I think. Maybe," she went on honestly, "I'm different now, too. When I thought Mother might want to marry Paul, I could only see it from our angle, how it would have messed things up for us."

"I thought of that, too," Penny agreed. "But I want her to be happy."

"So do I." Pam nodded. "I guess I'm not as selfish as

I used to be. Mother's got a right to a life of her own, just as you have, or I, or anybody else."

"Of course," Penny said. "But you weren't really selfish, Pam. I think it's just that we've both grown up enough to see things differently than we used to. We're more tolerant."

"Maybe that is it," Pam agreed.

"Take our attitude toward each other, too," Penny went on. "I'll admit I had you figured all wrong about school. I thought at first you were going to let Cade and that crowd you go with get you off the track. But now I can see you're following your own ideas. You seem to enjoy their company, but you're keeping up your grades in spite of their silly kidding and really getting a lot out of college."

"Thanks, pal," Pam said lightly. But Penny's words touched her just the same, made her feel warm and happy. It was nice to have Penny proud of her and coming right out and admitting it . . .

Joe Henderson, back from the University of Wisconsin, called Pam up and asked for a date the very first day she was home. But Randy didn't phone or drop in and Pam, after a couple of days, began to feel a little hurt by his attitude. Not that she didn't have plenty of dates; still, what a strange way for Randy to treat her. Pam couldn't understand it.

Then, at the skating party her old crowd held one night, she encountered Randy and the reason for his conduct became clear to her. He was with Laurie McGregor. And Laurie, Pam saw at once, must have taken full advantage of the fact that the colleges she and Randy were attending weren't too far apart. There was just a touch of the proprietary in Laurie's manner and the aura of happiness about her whenever Randy was near was almost dazzling. Randy himself wasn't quite so simple to figure out. He was as attentive to Laurie as any girl could wish and yet, once or twice, Pam thought his eyes lingered on her with a sort of quizzical intensity. As if, she thought, there were some unfinished business between them that was going to have to be settled one time or another.

She told herself, skating down the frozen lake with Joe Henderson's mittened hands holding hers, You could get Randy back if you liked. Even with Laurie looking at him with her heart in her eyes and acting as if she owns him.

But somehow there wasn't the old exciting challenge in the idea of winning a boy away from someone else, someone who wanted him as badly as Laurie had always wanted Randy. Let it ride, Pam told herself. And gave her full laughing attention to Joe as she dismissed the thought of Randy from her mind. . . .

Not entirely to Pam's surprise, Randy dropped in the next afternoon to see her. Penny was off somewhere or other with Mike and Pam had been helping Mother in the shop. But there was a mid-afternoon lull around the time of Randy's arrival, so Celia suggested that Pam take him upstairs and make him a cup of hot chocolate or something by way of hospitality.

The two of them sat on the low couch facing the fireplace in which a log fire smouldered and glowed. Mother's fragile old chocolate cups were set aside on the coffee table and almost all the cookies on the plate had been eaten up before Pam and Randy got around to anything very personal in the way of talk.

Randy asked rather abruptly, "How's your love life

these days? Lots of new men, I suppose? Your letters never sounded as though you'd changed any in that respect."

"I'm not so sure I haven't, though," Pam admitted with a faint smile. "I used to figure, the more the merrier. Now the field seems to have narrowed a bit."

She found herself telling Randy quite a bit about Cade, mentioning Jeff, too, in passing.

"It sounds," Randy said drily, "as though you might be getting a dose of your own medicine with this Cade. You used to make life pretty miserable for a lot of us, now I guess he's turned the tables."

Pam said, "I never meant to make you miserable, Randy. I like you a lot. I always did. I hope we're still friends."

"Oh, sure," Randy nodded. "We're friends. Why else would I be here?"

Pam told him and meant it, "I'm glad you and Laurie are back together."

"Laurie's a grand kid." Randy nodded. "We've had a lot of fun this year while we were away at school. Sometimes," Randy's grin was a little crooked, "what you think is second best works into something pretty wonderful. With Laurie, I know where I stand, what I can count on. That's more than I ever did with you, Pam. You couldn't help it, I guess, any more than this new man of yours, this Cade, can help keeping you guessing. One thing you were absolutely right about, though."

"What was that?" Pam asked.

"A few months apart have given us a different perspective, just as you figured they would. Or, at least, I can see things a lot straighter. I hope you get squared away with your problems, too, Pam. The main reason I dropped by today was to tell you I wasn't nursing any hard feelings or anything like that. I'll always be wishing you all the best. You know that."

"Thanks, Randy," Pam said a little thickly around the lump in her throat. . . ."

The holidays passed in a merry whirl for the twins. Penny and Mike went everywhere together. And Pam had more dates than she could keep up with. She didn't see much of Randy, except when they were thrown together at dances or parties. And on these occasions, there was the ease of old friendship between them. Their talk before the fire had dissipated all strain and tension.

On Christmas morning there was a great box of red roses from Cade and Pam's heart beat fast as she buried her face in their chill fresh fragrance. "Miss you," the card that accompanied them said simply. But Pam read enough special deeper meaning into it to make her happy, to start her counting the days until she and Cade would be together again.

One night when they were getting ready for bed, Penny asked Pam, "I suppose you've told Mother all about Cade—and Jeff?"

Pam nodded. "I've talked a lot about them both. Mother's so interested in all the things that have happened to us at school. And Cade is certainly the most exciting thing that's happened to me."

"She was asking me some more about him today," Penny admitted. "I guess all those roses made her wonder if you might be getting serious. I tried to be fair in what I said about him, Pam. But you know I don't like him very well."

Pam found herself leaping to Cade's defense. She had missed him, even in these busy, exciting vacation days, more than she liked to admit even to herself. Rather to her surprise, she had missed Jeff Moore, too. At school, she had come to take their quiet friendship almost for granted, but there were times, now that they were apart, when she recalled something he had said, some expression of his face, with a queer poignancy. But Penny liked Jeff, so there was no need of defending him to her.

Pam said, "You don't understand Cade. He's wonderful, really. Sometimes I wish I could get at whatever's troubling him, deep down inside."

"Even if you could," Penny said, "you couldn't change him. I wish he didn't mean so much to you, Pam. I don't think he's good for you."

"There you go," Pam said lightly, "worrying about me again. Just have fun and forget it. We've only got a couple more days at home and then it's back to the old grind. Might as well enjoy ourselves. . . ."

20 *The Celebration*

SCARCELY were the twins back at college when they had to begin studying hard for mid-semester exams. Everyone was in the same boat, which helped a bit. The rule of evening study period was strictly enforced around Grace Kirkland and social activities were held to a minimum.

"Honestly," Marylou Ritter moaned, "after all the fun and excitement of the holidays and being home and everything, it's just like dropping straight out of heaven into you know where!"

"The timing is pretty fiendish," Pam agreed.

Still, she reminded herself, in a little while the exams would be over and things would settle down to normal once more. She wasn't, actually, too worried about her grades. She had been more conscientious about her work in college than she ever had in high school, nor had she required so much help from Penny. During the past months a sense of personal responsibility, such as she had never experienced before, seemed to have developed in Pam. Maybe this feeling of being on her own, of having

165

to succeed or fail by her own efforts, or the lack of them, was all a part of growing up. Maybe it was maturity, too, that made her look back on some of her more scatter-brained escapades at high school with wonder and shame. There was the time she had persuaded Penny, against her twin's better judgment, to take a trigonometry test in her place. They hadn't been caught in their switch of identities, but Penny had felt so badly about the deception that Pam had found herself sharing her sister's remorse. Now she realized that she wouldn't even dream of asking Penny to do such a thing, her own sense of integrity wouldn't let her. Strange, the difference a few months' time could make in a person.

But there were other ways in which Pam hadn't changed so much. She still felt a quick thrill of pride to see other girls' eyes gleam with envy when she went out with Cade. She still loved to catch a note of resentment in Tip's or Marylou's voice as they told her, "I don't know what you've got that I haven't. How I'd love to have Cade give me that melting look he reserves for you!"

Once Marylou said, relaying the word to Pam that Cade had called up while she was out on a double date with Jeff and Mike and Penny, "I don't see why you waste time on Jeff Moore, when Cade's chasing you."

"I like Jeff," Pam told her. "He's real swell when you get to know him."

"But you like Cade better, don't you?" Marylou asked. "Or have you flipped your lid entirely?"

Pam smiled. "He's more distracting, shall we say? Jeff doesn't take my mind off my studying so completely. And with exams starting Monday—" she left it at that.

Marylou's eyes narrowed thoughtfully. "You wouldn't

be playing it very cagey, would you, pet? Keeping Jeff as insurance, so Cade wouldn't get too confident? Maybe some of us ought to start taking lessons from you."

Pam considered the matter with mock solemnity. "Shall I have my sign read, PAM HOWARD—LOVE LIFE CONSULTANT?"

There were times when she wasn't sure herself why she kept on going out with Jeff when she knew how bitterly Cade resented him. And yet—Pam faced the fact honestly—she knew she would miss Jeff if she stopped seeing him. Her blood might not race at his touch as it did at Cade's, still there was something between them that was strong and quiet. A bond of friendship, of liking, of mutual respect. Added together, what did these things equal? Pam wasn't sure. She knew Cade's kiss still made her feel weak with the rush of her emotions. But she couldn't compare it with Jeff's kiss, because Jeff hadn't kissed her. And that was another thing Pam didn't quite understand. In his own special quiet way, Jeff was almost as unfathomable as Cade.

Exam week had no more days than any other. And so, endless as it seemed, it was finally over. The mimeographed sheets of test questions were no longer stacked on every professor's desk, confronting you as you came into class. The atmosphere of uneasiness and foreboding lightened. Now that it was all over and too late to change an answer or alter a single grade, a kind of giddy aftermath settled over the campus. Even the gray sleety weather had no power to dampen spirits, or quell a kind of infantile rowdiness that led to all sorts of crazy pranks and nonsense.

But the faculty proved forbearing. Long experience

had taught them that the wave of silliness would pass. Besides, most of them were pretty busy grading test papers. So they ignored for the most part a rash of red hats on the dignified statue of Jonathan Harwood and the iron deer that somehow made its way one night from the courthouse lawn to the middle of the athletic field and the full size Confederate flag that startled all eyes one morning from the top of the campus flagpole.

The following Friday the mid-semester grades were handed out. And Pam was surprised and pleased to see how well she had done. Not so well as Penny; still her grades were quite satisfactory.

"Aren't you proud of me?" she asked Penny.

And Penny answered, "I certainly am. And I can't take any credit, either."

"Well, a little," Pam conceded, laughing, "but not as much as usual . . ."

Some of Pam's crowd decided to go in to the city that Saturday night and do all the gay spots by way of celebration. They would dine and dance and be merry, three couples including Pam and Cade.

"Not," Cade said wryly, "that I've got anything to celebrate. Two conditions to work off and barely passing on my other subjects. But what do I care?"

As Pam was dressing for her date that night, slipping into a black velveteen suit with glittery buttons and a fluff of white lace in the deep-scooped neckline, Penny said, frowning, "Pam, I wish you weren't going clear in to Cleveland tonight. The weather's so awful."

"Don't worry," Pam smiled at her. "We won't be out-of-doors much."

"But that long bus ride," Penny said. "And it's hard to get cabs in the city a night like this."

Pam felt a small guilty qualm at Penny's troubled tone. Against her own better judgment she had let Cade and the others persuade her that, in view of the weather and the fact that this was a very special occasion, it would be all right to use Cade's convertible and Bill Health's coupe tonight.

"Just this once, though," Pam had insisted. "I'm not setting a precedent or anything."

But she knew now, looking into her twin's anxious face, that it wouldn't reassure Penny to know that she meant to break college rules by riding in a car with a student who didn't have permission to keep one. So Pam contented herself with patting Penny's shoulder and telling her again not to worry.

"And you'll be back before one?" Penny asked. "You cut it so close last week-end, I never thought you'd make it."

"I'll do better this time," Pam promised . . .

Everyone was in high spirits during the bus ride in to the city. The vehicle overflowed with students, all bent on celebrating in one way or another, and there was much kidding and laughter. Even the middle-aged driver joined in.

"We'll really do the town tonight," Cade said when they reached the bus terminal.

"Make it a night to remember," Bill Heath seconded.

And all the others agreed.

They picked up Cade's and Bill's cars from the nearby garage where they kept them and then went on to their first stop, a smart hotel supper club. From that point on, it seemed to Pam, the evening was like one of those movie montages, with bright lights and obsequious waiters and fast-paced floor shows and soft dance music all shifting and melting into each other. It was all very gay and noisy as usual. From the big hotel clubs, they went on to dim-lit, smoky little night spots, where no one seemed to worry very much whether they were old enough to be buying liquor. Cade's identification card indicated he was over twenty-one and that seemed to smooth things over for all of them.

Pam didn't drink much, she didn't care for it. But Tip Flanders got pretty silly. And Cade, Pam realized, was drinking more than any of the other fellows. She tried to get him to slow down, but that only made him worse. And his mood was getting ugly and morose.

Someone noticed the time finally and they realized they'd have to head for the bus terminal at once, if they were going to get back to college before the one o'clock deadline.

"And we've got to make that!" Pam exclaimed, feeling anxiety rise in her. She gathered up her coat and gloves and tried to hurry the others.

But Cade argued, "Let's be late. Live dangerously."

"I'd like to," Terry Morris said drily, "but I can't risk another run-in with old Harrison. Step on it, kids."

The sleety rain had ended, they discovered when they reached the street. But it was slushy underfoot and a chill wind had risen.

Cade helped Pam into his car with exaggerated solici-tude, then turned to Tip and Terry, who were standing just behind him. "Go with Bill, will you?" he coaxed. "I've got things I want to talk about to Pam."

"Cade, no—" Pam began.

But the other couple, not caring whose car they rode in and preferring not to argue the matter with Cade, were already heading for Bill Heath's coupe.

"That wasn't very nice," Pam admonished Cade as he climbed in beside her and switched on the ignition.

"I'm not a very nice guy—sometimes." Cade chuckled, edging the car out from the curb. "You should know 'that."

He seemed more cheerful now, his belligerence gone. And his driving seemed expert enough, Pam noticed. Still, remembering how heavily he'd been drinking, she felt a faint uneasiness. But it was only a couple of miles to the garage and traffic was light. She relaxed more easily into the cushions.

Deep down inside, Pam felt relieved to have the gay night almost over. Somehow, she hadn't enjoyed it all as much as she had expected to. They had done the usual things, gone to all the glittering expensive places, but the customary sparkle seemed to have worn a little thin for Pam. Now why was that, she asked herself? True, Cade had been glum part of the time, but that often happened. And certainly all the others had been gay enough. She had been gay herself. But had there been, Pam wondered, something just a bit forced and unreal about all the noise and laughter? Had they been like people pretending to have a terrific time, just going through the motions? Or was she the only one? The question hung unanswered in her mind.

A thought struck her then and she asked, with a little

smile, "Didn't you tell Tip and Terry you wanted to talk to me? You've hardly said a word."

"We've got lots of time," Cade said drily. "The night's a pup."

"But we haven't—" Pam began. And then she stopped, staring out the window, a frown wrinkling her forehead. She had been so intent on her own thoughts she hadn't been paying much attention to where Cade was driving. Now she exclaimed, "Cade, where are we? This doesn't look like the right street for the garage."

"Why should it?" Cade's tone was calm. "It isn't."

Uneasiness caught at Pam's throat. "But you've got to get your car back. We haven't much time to make the bus."

"What would you say," Cade asked, "if I told you we're not going to take the bus? I feel like a ride tonight, a good long ride. We're going to drive all the way back to school."

"Cade," Pam's voice was sharp with dismay, "you can't do that! Think of the jam you'll be in about having your car here. And I'll be in a jam for riding with you."

"I've been in jams before," Cade said casually. "Haven't you?" He reached out to turn on the radio and dance music filtered softly into the car.

For a moment Pam said nothing, trying to think her way out of the nightmare situation, to decide what she could do.

Cade said, "If you're worried about what they'll say at school, we won't go back there. We'll just drive on and on and never come back."

"Cade, you're talking crazy!" Pam's voice shook.

"No, I'm not, baby," Cade denied, his tone almost crooning, but with a mounting excitement underneath. "I've just had the most terrific, star-spangled idea of my life! You know what we'll do? We'll stop somewhere and get married. And we'll never set foot on the Harwood campus again. Why should I stick around that crummy little joint working off conditions when I could be going on a honeymoon with you instead?"

21   *The Fantastic Night*

IN a way, Pam supposed, it was almost funny. If you could get your teeth to stop chattering and could shake off a sick sense of helplessness and revulsion, you might be able to appreciate the exquisitely horrible humor of the situation. Here was Cade, whom she had found so attractive, suggesting that they elope. Wasn't marriage the logical step when you were in love, as she had been almost sure she was in love with Cade? Wasn't a proposal what most girls dreamed of? Well, she had just had a proposal. True, it was on the casual side. "We'll stop somewhere and get married," Cade had said, almost as if he had been suggesting they stop somewhere and have a hamburger. But Cade was still Cade, good-looking, charming when he cared to be, attractive and wealthy. And a little drunk, Pam's thoughts added. Half-hysterical laughter rose in her throat, but she choked it back.

She disciplined her voice to quiet reasonableness, addressing Cade as she might have spoken to a willful child, instinctively sensing the danger of antagonizing him. "I don't think that's such a terrific idea."

"Why not?" Cade demanded. "Don't you want to marry me?"

A voice inside Pam shouted, No!

Aloud she said, "Well—not right now. For one thing," she tried to keep her voice from trembling, "I'm not suitably dressed for a wedding. 'The bride wore black'—how would that sound in the society columns?"

Cade laughed so uproariously that she began to fear the liquor he had drunk had affected him more than she'd realized. The wind rushing outside the warm little private world that was the car assumed an ominous sound in her ears. She wished he wouldn't drive so fast, but knew that if she asked him to slow down, pure perversity would make him speed faster.

Cade said, "Don't worry about your clothes. We'll buy you a wedding dress, white satin and lace and a long veil—"

"At this hour of the night?" Pam asked. "No, I've got a better idea. We'll drive back to Harwood and—"

"No we won't," Cade said flatly. "I'm through with Harwood and so are you. Only one good thing ever happened to me there—I met you."

"Cade—" Pam's voice broke with the anxiety building up within her, "please listen to me."

"Sure, baby, sure," he said mildly. A disk jockey's voice broke into the music and Cade told him, "Shut up, you," and switched to another station.

Pam said, "Please take me back to school, Cade. After that—well, I wish you'd stay on, too, for your own sake, but if you don't want to, it's up to you."

Cade was silent for awhile. Pam hoped that meant he was seriously considering what she had said. If she could just persuade him— She heard her voice, talking on and on, so sensibly and reasonably, and it was as if she listened from somewhere outside of herself, as if she were at once spectator and participant in the scene. This can't be happening, Pam thought, not to me, Pam Howard. I can't be sitting in a speeding car with Cade Venner, trying to talk sense into him, while the miles slip away outside and we leave the city and the suburbs behind and the houses get farther and farther apart.

Finally her voice ran down and she sat there, still and tense, her hands twisted together in her lap.

"Nothing doing," Cade said firmly. "I told you before, we're all washed up with school. Both of us."

"I'm not!" Pam said, forgetting to be quietly reasonable, unable any longer to keep the urgency of fear from sounding through her voice. "You've got to take me back! My sister will be worried sick—I'll be in such a jam—"

"Forget it," Cade told her. "We'll send Penny a wire in the morning and she can tell 'em all we're married and not coming back to their little two-bit college."

Tears spilled from beneath Pam's eyelids. Somehow, until this moment, her predicament hadn't seemed quite real. It had been like a bad dream, from which she felt she must surely waken, to find it all untrue and her fears unfounded.

But now she knew it was no dream. Cade's shoulder was solid against hers as they swung around a curve in the road. Pam shivered at the contact and pushed herself away from him. A sob caught in her throat and Cade glanced toward her briefly in surprise.

"What's the matter with you?" he demanded.

"I won't marry you," Pam cried, "whatever you say, or wherever you take me! You haven't any right to treat me like this! I want to go back to school."

Cade murmured soothingly, "Take it easy, baby. You're getting yourself all upset. We can't have that."

He slowed the car gradually, pulled over onto the hard shoulder of the road and stopped. "Come here," he said, his voice husky, his arms reaching out for Pam.

"No!" she gasped. And tried to twist away from him, to turn her face from his seeking lips. She braced her hands against his chest and pushed hard. But his mouth found hers despite her struggles and his kiss hurt her lips.

Pam's only response to his caress was sick revulsion. And when he let her go, her hand came up instinctively and struck him hard across the cheek.

She heard the sharp, furious intake of Cade's breath, his enraged voice growling, "Why you—"

Pam reached for the door handle, turned it. But Cade's hand jerked it shut again. And he held her there, squirming and helpless, as he told her, "Don't be a fool! You can't get out 'way out here in the country."

"I don't care where we are," Pam sobbed. "I hate you! Let me go!"

The car swerved back onto the road again before the hard grip of Cade's arm loosened. He said between set teeth, "I'll let you go all right, but not out here in the middle of nowhere. The next open filling station we pass, you're on your own. You can call your precious sister from there. You can yell to the school authorities. I'll be too far away for it to matter!"

Relief welled up in Pam at the finality of his voice.

"If you want some hot coffee," the middle-aged station attendant told Pam, "I got some in my thermos. My missus always fixes plenty for me these chilly nights."

"That would be good," Pam said dully.

She took the thick cup the man handed her and sipped the warm, too-sweet liquid gratefully. The crowded little room where she sat on an upturned crate was littered with odds and ends and garish with placards advertising oil and inner tubes and soft drinks. But it was warm and safe and the telephone booth in the corner had seemed an answer to Pam's prayers. The attendant hovered solicitously near her, his leathery face under a pushed-back cap anxious and mystified.

He said, not for the first time, "If I'd'a known what it was all about when you got outa that car, I wouldn't'a just let him drive off and leave you that way."

"I wanted him to go," Pam answered again, as she had the other times. "It's all right. I just wanted him to let me out where there was a phone, where I could call someone and wait. Please don't worry."

She had already explained as much as she had felt was necessary. She appreciated the man's kindness, but she didn't want to talk about it all any more. Her head ached and she felt dull and drowsy in the overheated room. If only Jeff would come—

Thinking of Jeff, a feeling of relief and gratitude rose in Pam. After Cade's car had roared off into the night, she had stumbled into the phone booth and then stood for a moment, hesitant, not knowing whom to call. Penny would have no way to get to her. She would have to explain Pam's predicament to the house mother at Grace Kirkland and there would be all sorts of excitement and upheaval. And the strange part, Pam had realized, staring at her wristwatch, was that she wasn't even late yet. It had been only twenty minutes after twelve.

Maybe, Pam had thought, the college authorities wouldn't have to know all that had happened, if she handled the situation right. This filling station, she estimated, couldn't be more than a few miles from Jeff's farm, where they had picnicked that Sunday. If she could get hold of Jeff and he would take her back to Harwood, she might still be able to make it by one o'clock.

And so she had put through a call to the Moore farm and luckily it had been Jeff's sleepy voice that answered.

Pam had said simply, "Jeff, this is Pam. I'm in a spot. Will you help me?"

And Jeff had answered, "Of course," without a second's hesitation.

Nor had he bawled her out, or asked a lot of time-consuming questions, as she explained as briefly as possible what had happened. He had just told her, "Be there in ten minutes. We'll get you back on time."

Pam finished her coffee and set the thick cup down. She glanced at her watch for the hundredth time. If Jeff hadn't underestimated— Her thought broke at the sound of a car stopping outside. She got up quickly and followed the attendant to the door. It was Jeff's old sedan and Jeff's familiar face, anxiously looking out.

Pam hurried toward him, her own face alight. Jeff opened the car door and she climbed in beside him, thanking the station man again for all his kindness. Jeff thanked him, too, and they started off.

Pam's breath went out in a long sigh of relief.

Jeff's jaw was grim as he reached down and gave her hand a hard squeeze. "If I ever get hold of that guy Venner—"

But Pam wouldn't let him finish. She begged, "Let's not talk about him, Jeff, please? Sometime I'll tell you all that happened. You deserve that, you've been so swell about—everything. But right now I don't even want to think about it—" Her breath caught in a little choked sob as she said shakily, "Oh, Jeff, I was so scared!"

"Sure you were," Jeff comforted. "But you're okay now."

His arm went around her shoulders in a brief, wonderfully heartening hug. Strength seemed to flow in some miraculous way from him to her, so that Pam straightened a little and her lips curved into an unsteady smile.

"Yes, I know," Pam murmured . . .

She was in her own room at Grace Kirkland at two minutes before one. After all that had happened, Pam could scarcely believe it was true. She had encountered Marylou briefly in the hall, but they had had only a chance for a whispered word or two.

"Where were you?" Marylou had asked. "Miss the bus?"

And Pam had whispered in reply, "Cade drove back. I'll tell you about it tomorrow."

"Oh, boy!" Marylou's brows had risen. "Fireworks!"

Pam had been glad there was no time then for further details. She got ready for bed in the dark, her fingers numb and clumsy with weariness, with the abrupt letdown of tension after the hectic hours just past. For a time she stood hesitant in the middle of the floor. Penny was asleep, of course, but Pam felt an irresistible urge to be near her just the same.

She moved quietly to the adjoining bedroom, feeling her way around the furniture to Penny's bed. She stared down at the sleeping form of her twin and presently Penny stirred, as though the finger of Pam's need had reached out and touched her.

"Pam?" Penny's voice was thick with sleep. "Is it you?"

Pam leaned down, whispering in her most coaxing tone, "Mind if I crawl in with you? I'm cold."

It was an old excuse, familiar from their childhood. Penny moved over and Pam slipped in under the covers with her. They lay there close together, as they had lain many times before, the mere nearness of their bodies a comfort to each other.

Penny yawned audibly, then murmured, still sounding more asleep than awake, "Pam, nothing's wrong, is there?"

"No," Pam reassured her softly. "Go to sleep."

She didn't want to go into it all now. She was too tired, too spent, for detailed explanations. And Penny's bed, with Penny warm beside her, was too exquisitely relaxing to stay awake in. She'd tell Penny all about everything tomorrow. She'd have a lot of explaining to do tomorrow, Pam realized, when it was discovered that Cade had left school. But even if the Dean had her up on the carpet, her only offense had been to ride with Cade in a car she had known was forbidden. She could be punished for that, still it could have been worse, Pam thought gratefully, so very much worse.

She realized that her friends were going to misunderstand her reason for turning toward Jeff from now on. Tip and Marylou and the others would think it was because Cade had gone. They would assume that Jeff was just second choice. But Pam found that she was no longer so concerned over what the others thought. She knew now what Jeff was. Tonight had taught her.

He was all the things Cade never could be, for all his devil-may-care attractiveness, his facile charm. Jeff was a rock to cling to, strength when you needed it, understanding with no questions asked. Jeff was someone quite wonderful, Pam told herself, when your eyes got over being dazzled by Cade and could see Jeff clearly, his full stature and maturity.

Maybe, she thought, I had to grow up a bit more to realize that, to really appreciate him.

Penny pressed, anxious despite her drowsiness, so closely attuned to Pam that she sensed some of her turmoil of spirit, "Pam, everything is all right, isn't it? You weren't late?"

"Everything's fine," Pam said soothingly. "Jeff got me back in time."

"Jeff?" Penny yawned again. "You mean Cade."

"Ummm," Pam murmured ambiguously, settling herself deeper into the pillow, closing her eyes as waves of sleep washed up around her.

There would be time enough tomorrow for Penny to find out exactly what she did mean.